THE LOST LANGUAGE OF CRAZY

THE LOST LANGUAGE OF CRAZY

Pamela Laskin

atmosphere press

To all of those who have made my story:

In memory of Solomon and Mary Laskin, Carl Laskin, Sylvia Novick and all the other Laskins and Reisers.

In memory of Gulliver Reiser, whose face always made me happy!

As always, to my husband, Ira.

To my children, Samantha, Craig, and Amanda, and to their children, who will tell their own stories
Precious Ella and Jacob

To Josh

"Memory" by Shara McCallum
June 30th, 2017, *The New York Times*

I bruise the way the most secreted,
most tender part of a thigh exposed
purples then blues. No spit-shine shoes,
I'm dirt you can't wash from your feet.
Wherever you go, know I'm the wind
accosting the trees, the howling night
of your sea. Try to leave me, I'll pin you
between a rock and a hard place; will hunt you,
even as you erase your tracks
with the tail ends of your skirt. You think
I'm gristle, begging to be chewed?
No, my love: I'm bone. Rather: the sound
bone makes when it snaps. That ditty
lingering in you, like ruin.

Selected by Terrance Hayes

"I have sometimes imagined my own sanity as resting on the surface of a membrane, a thin and fragile membrane that can easily be ripped open, plunging me into an abyss of madness, where I can join the tumbling souls whose membranes have likewise been pierced over the ages."

-Ron Powers, *No One Cares About Crazy People*

PROLOGUE

I was only two and a half when my mother disappeared
or died,
But what I remember is
that she loved beautiful boy things
such as fixing cars
and plumbing and she wrote poetry
under the name Stavan
though her name was Star.

She told me everyone has a story
even me.

FALL

CHAPTER ONE

"If I can't play the father, you can't use my play," I tell my teacher, Ms. Reise.

"You don't understand," Reise insists. "You entered this play into a competition, and it won. Part of the prize is to have the theater department do a production of your play. That was explained clearly in the entry information. There was nothing that said you get to pick a role for yourself."

"It shouldn't have won. It's not finished. It needs a new ending."

"But it did win!" Reise's eyes plead. "You can change the ending."

Reise is the middle school drama teacher, one of the best, though we get into disagreements sometimes. She takes her job very seriously!

Silence. We sit on it together. I can wait this out better than she can. Dad says I'm the most stubborn person he knows. Ms. Reise's crazy if she thinks otherwise.

"What's going on here? What's really behind this, Penelope?" she asks finally.

"Pilar. Remember I changed my name?"

Reise rolls her eyes. "Pilar."

"Nothing is behind it. I told you I want to play the dad. If I can do that, and you let me change the end, you can use it."

"You're the writer, not the actor. Performances are for our theater students. And besides, don't you think a boy should play the father?"

"No. I believe in color-blind and gender-blind casting."

I read this in the "Arts and Entertainment" section of my dad's *New York Times*. I was eleven at the time, but it sounded cool. It's the only part I like to read, even now.

Reise sighs. She knows she has lost. Inwardly, I beam, proud of my quick gender-blind, color-blind response. I really do believe in those things but I can't always get the right words out fast like that. Reise is used to quick-witted kids. After all, this is Middle School 55 in Brooklyn, school for the Gifted and Talented, mostly science geeks and freaks. A few Goths and wannabe artists. People with names like Gatsby, Brooklyn, Marigold.

"It's not being performed till late November or early December. Why don't you think about it?" Reise presses on.

"You don't understand."

"No, I don't, Penny."

"Pilar," I correct her again.

"Pilar. I don't know why you insist on using a different name."

I like changing my name every year. This started in sixth grade, and now that I am in eighth, I have found the perfect name for me—for now. I know this seems crazy, but it works, and everyone sort of adapts.

"Okay, whatever. Can you at least think about it? You can finish it with the ending you like."

"I'll think about it." I'll have to think about it because I have no idea what the ending should be. I only know that the play isn't finished.

She nods and I hurry from the room, eager to leave the drama behind.

Where Happy Little Bluebirds Fly

Welcome to my blog, whose name is "Over the Rainbow." You can follow me on this or on Twitter, @Overtherainbow. I named my blog this because I am a super fan of *The Wizard of Oz* and I think there is a lot that can be learned about life in that movie. This is a free, safe space where we can talk about anything. "Where happy little bluebirds fly."

I am Pilar, also known as Penelope. Some people call me Penny, though I correct them. There are people who change shoes often, but that is not me. I prefer my plain, white Keds. What I do like to change, though, is my name, maybe once a year, since a new name helps me figure out who I am supposed to be at any given time. Right now, I am using the name my Spanish teacher gave me, Pilar. It is taken from the Virgin Mary, which means nothing to me, so I make believe it means strength. I am stronger than people think I am!

The Wizard of Oz isn't all I will be talking about on this blog. I want to tell you about all that I see and do. If Toto helps us make sense of it, that's even better. I think of myself as a writer, so sometimes I'll talk about my writing. Other times I will talk about my friends, family, and people I know.

CHAPTER TWO

"So, what happened?" Zeina asks as we come out of the building at dismissal time.

We blend with the crowd of departing students until we branch off to a side street that fewer kids use on their way home.

"Why did Reise want to see you?"

Zeina and I don't have any classes together after lunch, so I haven't had a chance to tell her about my meeting yet.

"Oh, okay. I won some stupid award for a play I submitted."

"Oh my God, oh my God. What award? That is so exciting. I can't believe it!"

Zeina has been in this country over two years, and she's become so American—I mean, so *American*. She thinks awards are the best. She dresses like a Muslim-American girl, though lately she has been pushing things, replacing her long skirts with jeans. She's even considered taking off her headscarf, her *hijab*, but so far, it's all talk. I hope she doesn't. She wears the prettiest scarves in swirling colors that highlight her blue eyes. I can't imagine my friend dressed any other way, so I guess you could say I like it; the headscarf is just a small, characteristic part of Zeina, as far as I'm concerned. Zeina doesn't like it. She complains that people give her funny looks and treat her like she's not an American because of how she has to dress. I get that. Being treated weirdly because people think you're different is super uncomfortable.

One of the nice things about Zeina is how happy she gets when good stuff happens to her friends. She is all but jumping up and down.

"It's an award, Pilar," she says. "It's an honor."

"The award thing is sort of complicated," I say.

"Why?"

"The play is *not* finished. At least not in a way I'm happy with."

"But it won," Zeina points out. She's like, what's the big deal? "They picked your play, so obviously it's better than you think it is."

"Yeah. But..."

I'm not even sure why I entered this dumb competition. I wrote this play about my Dad and me. It's about how one year there was a blizzard. Dad and I were snowed in, alone. It's all true, though I exaggerated some things like the size of the blizzard. But the part that was true was how we talked about my mother, who died when I was very little. Dad told me how much she loved me and how she fought through her cancer but eventually had to give in. It ended with Dad and me holding onto each other and singing "Somewhere Over the Rainbow," from our favorite movie, *The Wizard of Oz*.

It's very heartwarming. And we really did talk about my mother and sing. The thing is, I remember my Mom at times, and sometimes they are warm memories, mostly of her singing to me. She liked to sing, and she also liked to dress the same way my Dad dressed. I wonder why. I wonder if this is something real—or if I imagined this. My memories are mostly vague. But I should have waited to hand it in. The thing is, I couldn't, because the submission deadline was up. It was now or never. Still, as the days passed, something about the play began to feel wrong. I can't tell you what or why; it just wasn't right. Maybe it was too sweet.

"It needs a different ending, but I don't know what the ending should be," I tell Zeina.

"A win is a win. If the judges thought the ending works, then it works."

Sometimes she makes things sound so easy, so uncomplicated. Not me. To me life is like the rose—as I said in my blog—layered, complex. (I remember that Shrek said that he was like an onion, many-layered—but I definitely do not want to think of myself as an onion. Too smelly, and I try to never make people cry.)

"I have to eat something," I tell her. My stomach rumbles and my mind are cloudy, the way it gets when I'm hungry.

"You had better eat. That belly rumble was like thunder. I'll sit and watch you!"

Yikes—during Ramadan, she doesn't eat until the night, but it is *not* Ramadan, so I can't figure it out. She is skinny, so thin that her pants drag on her. I don't exactly feel comfortable pigging out in front of her. But maybe something is wrong; I will have to watch her!

"Why aren't you eating?"

"I'm not hungry." Her body gets all uncomfortable looking. I have to stop.

"So, your play won," Zeina says as we continue walking, prompting me to continue my story. "Why did Reise have you in her office for so long? You were there all through lunch."

"We don't have to eat," I say, knowing she will not.

"Just tell me what happened!" Zeina cries.

I want to talk about why she is not eating, but the firm set of her jaw and her furrowed brows tells me I have to stop. I've seen this fierce expression before. She will not be distracted from getting her answer.

"After Reise told me about the award and how she wanted the play performed on the day of the awards celebration, I told her only if I could play the lead, and she gave me a flat-out no."

"I understand. It's a story about your life. You're the best person to play yourself."

"Not exactly," I say. "I want to play the dad part."

"What?!" Zeina cries. "Why?"

I shrug. "It's more interesting. I already know what's in *my* mind. I want to explore what's inside him."

Zeina studies me. She narrows her eyes and purses her lips. "That's deep, Pilar."

I'm relieved because I was expecting an argument or maybe even ridicule. I should have known better. Zeina gets me. That's why we're so close.

"Why won't she let you play the father?" she asks.

"She said, first of all, they have a theater department, and second of all, boys should play boys and girls should play girls. So, I'm not letting her use the piece, since she won't let me play the dad."

"Kids will make fun of you if you play the dad. You know that, right?"

I shrug. "Let them."

Some kids might make online cracks. Most of them are used to me going my own way. It wouldn't exactly be a shock.

"Maybe Reise will change her mind," Zeina suggests.

"She won't. But I'm just as stubborn. Neither will I!"

A Victim Of Disorganized Thinking

The Wizard of Oz tells the Cowardly Lion that he is a victim of disorganized thinking. I can relate to that. Maybe that's my problem, too. Maybe my thinking is simply disorganized. I *have to* find the right ending for my play, I really do. I wish I knew where it was going, but I don't. I have no idea what its future is. Like, if there is no mom in my play, why doesn't my dad get a wife in real life? Really, what's his story? Maybe if he brought one home, I wouldn't even know what to do with her! Should a man who seems disinterested in a wife in *real* life have a wife in my play? I am having a hard time figuring out what to do as a writer.

I need to figure out what this play is really about. Is it about my mother's death? Is it about how my mother's death has messed up my dad and me? Has it messed us up? Maybe we're just fine without her. It is about how I miss my mother. Do I miss my mother? Are we happy? Or maybe we are totally screwed up and don't even know it. Maybe the Dad in the play needs a wife, even though the Dad in real life will not get one. The play just isn't finished. I can feel that in a way I can't describe. It needs something more.

CHAPTER THREE

"What's going on at school?" Dad asks.

"What?"

I am so stunned by his question that the Rice Krispies fall off my spoon and land all over the floor, the table, my dad. My dad just never asks about school, since he knows I am such a good student. He usually asks about my friends or my writing, two things which he knows are important to me. Dad laughs at the mess and mops up Snap, Crackle, and Pop with his napkin.

"I'm just curious."

"Rat Reise called you. Didn't she?"

"Who?"

"Ms. Reise, Queen of Drama."

"I thought *you* were the Queen of Drama, Sarah Bernhardt."

"Who's she?" I ask Dad.

"Sarah Bernhardt is dead, but at one time, sometime in the 1800s, maybe the early 1900s, I think, she was an actress—the Jewish Queen of Drama."

Jewish. Dad always has to get that in somehow, some way. He *constantly* asks me if I'm practicing for my bat mitzvah, which is three months, three days, and fourteen minutes away. He asks at least three times a week.

"What's the story, Dad? Why are you asking about

school?"

He throws up his hands. "You got me. Yes, Rat Reise called."

"About what, this time?"

Reise sometimes calls home. Don't misunderstand, I'm not one of those detention kids or anything, but I'm also not one of those quiet-as-a doormat kids, either, so there is always a call—or three. I suspect she picks on my house to call because there's no mom. She calls this "being proactive on behalf of the student." Ugh!

"Was it about the play?"

"Yes. Penny, why—"

"Pilar!"

"Okay. Have it your way, Pilar. I don't understand why..."

"It's *my* play, Dad," I start to shout, "and it's not even finished, and she won't let me play the lead. She doesn't get that the play is mine. MINE!"

I'm mad. Angier than I even knew. All I did was hand in the stupid play too soon. Now they won't give it back to me. They won't let me have any say in what happens to it next. This isn't fair. It's not right! Somehow my shouts turn to sobs.

"Penny...Pilar, it's not that big of a deal," Dad says, coming around the table to hug me. "You wrote a great play and they want to see it performed. You should be proud and happy. I have a really strong feeling that you'll regret it if you don't have this play performed. Believe me! This is a big honor and you don't want to let this chance pass by."

It feels great to be crying in my Dad's arms. I don't cry that often, since I am tough as nails. At least I want to be.

Really, inside I'm mush. Everything affects me. Zeina once told me I was "too sensitive." So, like the Little Prince's rose, I've grown some thorns.

I can't stop the stupid tears from flowing. At last, Dad suggests his cure-all when things get bad or scared or just plain overall sucky—*The Wizard of Oz*. That part of my play is exactly accurate.

"Okay," I agree with a sniffle, wiping my runny nose on a dinner napkin.

We sit side-by-side on the couch, watching TV. Where did I get my love of theater? From Dad, of course, who has introduced me to musicals since forever. Before long, Toto and Dorothy are off, spinning their way out of tornado-torn Kansas, and plunking down in Oz with Munchkins and lions and tigers and bears, oh my! And, before you know it, we are singing off-key, "Somewhere over the rainbow, way up high, there's a land that I heard of, once in a lullaby."

Blog #3 www.Overtherainbow@blogspot.com

I Haven't Got A Brain...Only Straw

That's how I've been feeling–like a straw-brain. The start of a new school year has got me feeling fried in my head. There is so much to remember, so many forms to fill out, so much new work to get a handle on. Just having to remember which classroom I have to get to at what time is a challenge.

It's fall, suddenly—the t-shirts come off, the sweaters go on, the leaves drop in spiraling swirls onto the ground. Dad is calm for a little while, so he leaves me alone. No one bugs me about the play—not even Dad or Ms. Reise, or even my friends, Calvin, Ava, Ruth, Johnny, or Zeina—some of whom REALLY want parts in my play that is not even finished.

There are only days of school, sometimes babysitting to make some money, hanging out with friends. I call these times quiet times. There are not too many of these, since I am not a quiet person inside. Dad and I watch *The Wizard of Oz—TWOO*—again and again and again. Sometimes he reminds me to practice my Torah portion, but I try to ignore him. I have been dreaming a lot, blog, but can't remember in the morning if they are good or bad dreams, so not sharing with you at all! I know my Mom liked to talk. Would she have helped me with my bad dreams? I wish I could remember them. I would, believe me—if I only had a brain.

CHAPTER FOUR

"Cleaning day," announces Dad, like the Cartoon Network character, Fred Flintstone. He can sometimes be really annoying.

"Not!"

"What?"

He is in my face, while I'm busy inhaling a whole bowl of Honey Nut Cheerios. "I have plans!"

"Penny, other than finishing your play or practicing for your bat mitzvah, what is so important?"

"Pino's Pizza with my friends for lunch. "

"That's not a whole day!"

"Neither is cleaning. Oh, and that apron *has* to go!"

Dad looks down at his apron, a kind of vintage *Beauty and the Beast*. The roses are so ridiculous that I feel like pulling the thing right off of him.

"I like my apron. Anyway, there's nobody here to see it."

Right, Dad, that's me. I'm nobody. And you? You're Mr. Clean. That's what I call him, and it has sort of caught on in the family. The thing is, he is crazy clean, as in everything is shining and polished and empty, empty, empty. Aside from my room, it seems like no one lives here. My room is the opposite. Hey, I am a writer, so I save clippings from newspapers, and I have multiple drafts of everything I write. I even save what I don't like, since you never know when I might like it again.

"I'll clean soon, but I have to work on my play a little."

He nods his head yes. I knew this would impress him!

I never want to clean. In fact, the more Dad insists on cleaning, the more I am thrown into my play. His insistence on cleaning becomes my insistence on writing. So, when I go up to "take a break," I start to work on my play.

Dad: Why aren't you cleaning your room?

Piper: There is so much junk in here that I don't know where to begin.

Dad (Looking exasperated): What is your problem with cleanliness?

Piper: It's like you've emptied the house of life, Dad.

Dad: What does that mean?

Piper: There is so little clutter that I need a messy room just as a hideaway.

Dad: I don't understand you!

Piper: Of course not!

My writing bleeds into my life.

"What are you doing, Pilar?"

Wow, he called me Pilar without being asked; that's a first. "I am just finishing up my closet."

Dad has a hard time with my name changes. He thinks I am weird. Or he is split. Part of him admires my creativity, but since he is not a creative person, he really does not get me.

Lie. But aren't storytellers all liars, playing with the truth?

"Good...good. And if you're doing the laundry after, don't forget to use the Shout."

"Sure."

Twenty minutes later, my wash is still sitting in a pile while I lean on the closed washing machine, looking over what I've just written. It's not bad, but does it move the story along, or is it only filler? Am I making progress or am I stalling until the idea I'm searching for hits?

Rub-Rub Here! Rub-Rub There!

Here's a secret. I don't mind doing the laundry. Isn't that crazy? Today washing the sheets has got me thinking. Dad reminded me to use the Shout, but I don't want to. The stains make the sheets interesting. Laundry is like a mystery novel and the stains are the clues.

Reise, who every so often accidentally says something interesting, was talking about something called a palimpsest. A palimpsest means a piece of paper or some other thing that you wrote on that you tried to erase, maybe by washing it off, but you can still see that someone wrote on it, and maybe even make out some of what it said. Like on a blackboard, when you walk into the room and you can still read the lesson from the class before yours, because the eraser didn't completely take it away. The ghost of the words is there—you can see it if you try. The traces never really disappear.

My sheets...my history, a thousand nights of dreaming. This brownish splotch is from a time my period surprised me by coming on in the night. (I'm still never sure when it's going to appear.) When I write in bed, I always leave an inkblot. Older sheets sometimes have yellowed pee stains. If I caused those as a child, I don't remember, but *somebody* peed the bed. I recall my mom never got mad at me when I peed in the bed. I'm working on a book of poems about laundry and it's called *Secrets of the Sheets*.

Here's the first poem in it. I hope you like it, blog, and all my followers.

Sheets Talk

Sheets tell hidden stories
that are often tear-stained
and sometimes filled with blood.
Ink-stained sheets reveal
truths the writer could not
       express with words.
The self unfolds
       in the secrets of the sheets.

CHAPTER FIVE

"Hey, P! Wait up!" Johnny calls to me just as I'm leaving my locker.

I let him get away with calling me P because he always says it with his intense indigo-blue eyes twinkling with approval. You would think, though, that he would be a little more sensitive to name changes since, not that long ago, Johnny went by the name Jasmine, until he announced that he was no longer female and wished to be called Johnny. This happened in sixth grade; Jasmine became Johnny over Christmas break, and since everyone knew Jasmine never liked being a girl, didn't *feel* like a girl, it was never a big deal to my friends. He reaches my locker, panting from his sprint down the hall.

"What up, P? Finish that play yet?"

"Not yet," I say. He falls into step with me as I move on down the hall.

"Well, get it done, would ya? What are you waiting for?"

"Why do you care so much?"

"Because I want the dad part in the play so everyone will realize I'm a guy."

"Johnny, everyone knows you're a guy."

"I won't *really* be, until I take those stupid hormones."

"Forget about *me* taking my time with the play. What

are *you* waiting for? Just get the hormone shots already! You've only been talking about it for two years, since you chopped off your hair. Everyone knows you're not Jasmine anymore. I don't even remember what Jasmine looked like."

That's not entirely true. I do remember Jasmine's long black hair, now shaved at the sides but still full and wavy up top—same slightly upturned nose with a light spray of freckles across the cheeks. Jasmine was a pretty girl and now Johnny is a completely adorable boy, but in a very different way.

"I don't know about all that hormone stuff," Johnny says.

He's off again—same old, same old. We have had this conversation literally five-hundred times. It always ends with Johnny saying he's not ready—yet. And his parents, especially his dad, would be really mad at him.

"Then don't," I say. I am so not in the mood for the hormone debate.

"Why are you so cranky?" He points his phone at me and goes into his talk show host routine. "We are here today with the distinguished author Pilar Lasky, who is about to tell us why hormones have *her* going haywire. Ms. Lasky, how does it feel to be menopausal at the age of thirteen?"

"Cut it out," I say. "You better not have that camera on. And I am *cranky,* as you put it, because everyone is bugging me about finishing the play, as if I know the ending."

"Okay, but when you *do* finish it, please convince Reise to let me play the dad."

"Sorry. I want to play the dad," I tell him.

"But you're a girl."

I feel a flash of annoyance but let it pass.

"Besides, didn't Reise already tell you no?"

"Uh-huh. Yes, because I'm a girl, but that's not fair."

"Well, that's no problem for me."

Johnny and I look at each other. He really is cute. Too bad he knows it. He shoots me his irresistible 'Aw, come on' smile.

"You know I'd make a great dad, P. Come on! Admit it! I'm a natural-born actor."

"I've never seen you act in any of the school plays."

"That's why I have to start now. You're my ticket to stardom!"

I shove him lightly on the shoulder. "You're so crazy! I have to go to class."

*

That night, I go home and Google Sarah Bernhardt. I learn the most interesting fact: *Sarah Bernhardt traveled America performing, and she often played male roles: various soldiers, generals, and male heroes. Her most famous male role was as the lead in Shakespeare's* Hamlet, *Prince Hamlet, himself.*

Actually, Shakespeare has lots of plays where men pretend to be women and women pretend to be men. In fact, *all* the roles—male and female—were played by men at first. So they had men pretending to be women who were pretending to be men. Wow.

Then I remember that Peter Pan is always played by a woman in the musical. As a kid I sometimes watched the old version with Mary Martin and the newer one with

Cathy Rigby. Aha! The idea of me playing the dad isn't so crazy, after all.

I cut and paste the Wikipedia article about Sarah Bernhardt into an email that I send to Reise's school inbox. I also attach the one about female leads in Peter Pan, just to really make the point.

I'm Melting! Oh, What A World! What A World!

It is October and I am sweating to death, which is a crazy expression, since I don't know of anyone who ever died from sweating. The truth is, it should not be eighty degrees in October. I mean, it's fall, and no one would know that, so I think it is absurd when people discuss climate change and they say it is a hoax. My father is a scientist, and if you are a scientist you have to know that icebergs should not melt in the winter; we should not have so many hurricanes. We had a president who did not believe in this stuff. You'd think people would have learned after that horrible storm, Hurricane Sandy, actually closed our subways and left people without power for weeks. Now that is scary, and there's no getting around the truth that our weather is schizophrenic. My father always uses that word—by which he means crazy. That is what my dad says and I really kind of believe him! My Dad *DOES NOT LIKE* crazy people.

CHAPTER SIX

"I have to come to your house today," I tell Zeina during lunch in the cafeteria, where I've decided to try carrots for the first time.

"Why do you always say that when I always tell you no?!"

What she says is true. I have never—not once—stepped inside the basement-level apartment where Zeina lives. She's been to my place a zillion times, so I think I can safely say it would be more than fair if she would let me into her apartment this one time when I really need a place to hide out.

"I can't go to Hebrew school today. I'm not prepared. I can't tell my Dad that, so I need to be somewhere for an hour. Pino's doesn't like it when you just order water and hang out."

"So order a pizza," Zeina suggests.

"It doesn't take an hour to eat a slice of pizza."

"Then order two."

"C'mon," I whine. "I just want to come over for an hour. Why are you being so mean to me?"

No answer.

There is an issue here, but she won't say what it is, and that's for sure.

"Why is your house always off limits?" I ask.

"Let's go to Pino's and I'll explain."

"So you are eating?"

"Shit, why are you bothering me?"

It freaks me out to hear Zeina speak this way, since she is such a good soldier—a rule follower, not someone who curses. She has always loved her Middle Eastern traditions; she really loves and respects her family, so this all feels a little too crazy. Her saying "shit," I mean.

But when we get to Pino's, she doesn't tell me why I can't come to her house; she doesn't share anything. She eats quickly and quietly with her eyes gazing down on the floor. She eats two bites of the pizza. She is *forcing* herself to eat. I'm more creeped out that she has been cursed. What is going on?

"What's up, Zeina?" I ask.

"Nothing," she says. She swallows hard in one gulp. "Nothing."

Folding my arms, I stare at her. She squirms under my heavy gaze. Just like with Reise, I'm not backing down. I'm going to get the answer from her somehow.

"Tell me," I insist.

"No."

"Why not?"

"You'll be mad."

"I won't. Just tell me."

"I can't go to your bat mitzvah."

"What? Are you kidding me? That's crazy!"

"See?! You're mad!" Her eyes fill up with tears. "It's my dad. You know my dad."

"Actually, I don't. I've never met him. Remember?"

Zeina's tears roll down her cheek and I realize this is *not* the time to be sharp with her.

"I'm sorry," I say sheepishly.

And then she can't hold back any longer. The dam spills over—how she can't stand being home, how insanely strict her dad is, how he doesn't want her to mingle with people outside of her culture, how he had wanted her to go to an Islamic school, and how they didn't have the money—and how angry this made him.

"And," Zeina adds. "He is so embarrassing. He get these things in his head like he does not want me to go to a bat mitzvah. He doesn't even understand them. Plus, he hates big parties. He is just too odd and nothing he says makes any sense. I can't take it! I can't take him." The heavy crying starts all over again.

*

That is so odd that Zeina's dad is so opposed to big parties. It is, after all, my PARTY! It is really weird. I kinda understand how upset she was... Her mother doesn't seem to feel this way, though I could be wrong. She might simply be hiding it. I can't believe that, though. It feels very uncomfortable, wondering whether Mrs. Mohammed also doesn't want Zeina to go to my bat mitzvah. She always smiles at me when I see her at the supermarket. Oh, God. This is like *Romeo and Juliet*, only with best friends.

I have to get a grip on this. So Zeina can't come to my bat mitzvah. It's okay. I can get through it without her. And who cares if her father doesn't like big parties? He's not the one who is important to me. Zeina is my friend, always and forever. That's what counts.

Are You A Good Witch Or A Bad Witch?

I don't really remember much of my mother before she died, though I have dim memories of a large woman in overalls. Sometimes she sang to me. She had a sweet voice. She had liked show tunes, like Dad, and sometimes she sang me "My Little Girl" from *Carousel*. I feel like maybe I was one. I recall she had a belly laugh. But as I got older—closer to two—this woman with a sweet voice seemed to smile less.

Lately I have been having dreams about her and all of them involve knives. My mother is standing over my crib and there is a knife in her hands. Now that seems crazy, since I must have been less than two years old and, yet, that image is sharp. There is often more than one knife, and more than one image of her with the knife; however, there is never blood, never violence, never pain, just the knife, clear and sharp and brutal. But it doesn't feel as brutal as you might imagine. I can picture my mother's smile and the knife or knives, but nothing else. My mother's smile is huge and it glistens, too. Like the blade of the knife. The smile is only there when the knives are there.

CHAPTER SEVEN

"I really hope you do this play," says Johnny as he devours his pizza.

"Like I told everyone, it is not even finished."

"It's November, P. Just finish the stupid play." He shouts this and everyone in the pizzeria turns to look at us, including some kids from school.

"Could you keep it on the down-low?" I hiss.

"What? What did I say?" Johnny challenges in the same loud voice.

More stares. I know I'm turning red. I can feel the burn.

"Let's go," I say, standing.

We hit the street and walk on in silence. When we are on 4th Street and 7th Avenue, a few blocks away, Johnny turns to me.

"What's the matter with you?" he demands angrily.

"I don't need everyone knowing about my play," I reply.

"Oh, like anyone cares," he says. "Everything is not about you, P."

"*You* care about the play! Obviously!"

"I told you why! I am a boy for real. I need everyone to get that. If I can't play the dad, then write a different guy part for me."

"There's no other guy character in the play. I'm not going to make one up just so you can make some big announcement to the world. Everyone can see that you're a guy. I know that you're really a guy," I tell him.

"No, you don't. You think I'm *pretending* to be a boy."

Suddenly, Johnny presses his body against mine—hard, so hard, I can barely breathe, and we're kissing. It's weird to be kissing Johnny. It's also scary; plus, it's not what I want. I knew Johnny had a crush on me, but I thought it was in check; plus, I thought he understood it was not what I felt, not ever.

"Stop it!" I tear away from him. "I didn't ask for that!"

"I've always had a crush on you, and I know you like boys, so if you really thought I was a boy, it wouldn't be such a big deal. There's no reason for you to be giving me the swerve except that you don't buy me as a guy."

And then he walks away, his shoulders hunched, his head down. Maybe he's right. Maybe I don't know anything. I love Johnny—he is very cute and sweet and everything a friend should be. But isn't there a possibility for a friendship to grow into a love interest? It is possible that I won't let it go there, since I am limited. Or am I scared? I am not sure. Maybe, Johnny is right—I am like everyone else, uncomfortable with his transition into becoming a guy. I mean, I hardly remember him as Jasmine. I cannot imagine I have that "bias" toward him. Johnny is a *HIM*—it is the only way I think about him. I don't think so, but lately, I do not know myself. I question Zeina's thinness. I question why Johnny did what he did— and why I reacted the way I did. I am filled with doubt and uncertainty.

*

That night I lie on top of my bed with the books I need for homework scattered around me. Occasionally, I pick one up, but I quickly put it down. I can't stop thinking about what happened with Johnny. I keep seeing his face as he called me out for liking boys, but not liking him. I don't think that was very fair. I don't like every boy I see, not in *that* way. Even if he had been born a boy, I still might not like him in *that* way.

But Johnny has shared that he was never a girl. Even when he was three, four, he knew he was a boy, and he told his parents, too, but they didn't understand. Do I understand? Now when I look at him, I really see a boy, but I do remember him as a girl, and maybe it still feels weird to me. This is a journey, to figure out myself and also those I love.

It's not as though I haven't obsessed over a guy, because I have. In a big way. When I crush, I crush hard! It's all I can think about. When I liked Alex Rogers last May, I walked the long way around to every class just to pass his locker as many times as possible hoping to get a look at him. He never even noticed that everywhere he was, there I was. He looked right through me as if I were invisible. At that same time, Jason Everly kept leaving me little gifts like gum and bookmarks and anything else he could slide into my locker. I never saw him do it, but my friend Ava, who has the locker next to mine, saw him and told me. He wrote his initials on every little offering. Jason is a nice kid but I didn't feel excited by his presence. I didn't long to be with him—not like I longed to be near Alex Rogers, who made my heart race just by appearing.

What makes one person thrilling and another person not? Movie reviewers say movie stars who play romantic movie scenes together have "good chemistry" or "no chemistry." So why did I feel super chemistry with Alex when he couldn't even see me? Was it because I was a grade below him? Was he feeling chemistry with some other girl? Why did *I* like *him* so much? I hardly knew him but I thought he was so adorable. He used some soap or something that smelled like pine trees. It got to me. It was like I needed to get close enough to smell him. Now, that's weird! I know! But people do stuff like that when they're in the grip of crazy love.

Now I can't stop picturing Johnny stomping away, all mad. I truly like Johnny. I would even say I love him, as a friend—when he's not being obnoxious. Why do you love someone one way, and not in the other? Johnny is cute. I like to hang out with him. I just don't feel that "thing" that you're supposed to feel, though. Attraction? I'm attracted to all my friends, as people. It's not the same.

Underneath all my anger, all my sadness about hurting Johnny's feelings, and my embarrassment about everybody seeing us yelling at each other in the street—and then Johnny grabbing at me like a big macho character or something—there is also this big, empty disappointment.

My first kiss. I dreamed about it so long, and it was always so beautiful in my dreams. And now—this.

To be honest, I kind of miss being obsessed with a guy. But at the moment there's no one I'm crushing on. I don't even think about Alex anymore. Next year, when I'm in high school, if I see Alex again, will I feel the same, or was it just a crush that has passed? What if his mom changed

soaps and he smells like almonds instead of pine? If he
smells like almonds will I still think about him day and
night? It's all so confusing! It could really drive a person
nuts.

An Awful Lot Of Talking

How did I end up with Leviticus when my birthday is in September? I was supposed to have my bat mitzvah around my birthday—September 14th—but my grandma got sick, first a cold, then pneumonia. And shortly after, my Zayde had to go into the hospital to get a pacemaker.

According to Jewish tradition, when a girl or boy goes through this rite of passage, they are given a portion of the Torah to read—in Hebrew, yuck!—but also to analyze. The portion I was supposed to get was much easier; I do not even recall the name, but I do know it was not so philosophical and complex.

Do I want to go through this? Sure, I love being center-stage, but I'm not so sure this time. The instructions for Leviticus emphasize ritual, legal and moral practices, rather than beliefs. They reflect the worldview of the creation of the story of Genesis, and God's wish to live with humans. It says that faithful performance of sanctuary rituals can make that possible if people avoid impurity and sin.

What is impurity? What is sin? It beats me. Is it impure that Johnny tried to kiss me? Hey, c'mon—it's what people do. How can you talk about God and sin in the same breath? This seems crazy, for when it comes down to love—what is sinning, really? I really WANT to be kissed by a boy, but Johnny does not feel like the one I wanted.

In *The Wizard of Oz*, Dorothy asks Scarecrow how he can talk if he doesn't have a brain. He replies, "Some people without brains do an awful lot of talking." Sometimes I feel as if that's me. I'm always talking or writing, and the more I do, the less I understand. Am I one of those brainless talkers?

CHAPTER EIGHT

It's been three days since that kiss, and Johnny won't even look at me. He turns in the opposite direction whenever we encounter each other. I desperately need to explain that I want us to be friends, even though I'm not attracted to him in that way, but he won't give me the chance. I text him to meet me in the school lobby at lunchtime. I'm surprised but happy to see him there.

"Johnny, I'm glad you're here," I say, walking toward him. "We have to talk about the other day when—"

"Face it, P! You didn't want to kiss me because you knew me when I was a girl."

"No!" I say. "That's not it!"

"You're lying. Don't talk to me anymore."

That stings.

He shakes his head as if to call me pathetic, then swings around toward the cafeteria without once looking back at me. I'm all over the place—sad, mad, confused. I feel guilty and I'm furious that he's making me feel that way. I don't know anything these days. How is this all *my* fault?

One thing I *do* know is I am *not* supposed to go to Zeina's house for some reason, but I can't stay away. I need to pick her brain on the Johnny situation, but Zeina has been out of school for the last three days. She's not answering my texts—all twelve of them. What if she is really, really sick? I've called and texted, called and texted. No reply. On the third day of this, I ring her bell. An eye at the peephole, and then I hear the scrape of the chain being unfastened on the other side of the door. Zeina opens the door. Instead of one of her colorful scarves, she wears her plain green hijab and a high, black turtleneck shirt and black pants.

"What are you doing here?" she asks.

"You were out of school for three days, and you didn't answer my texts or my calls. I expected to find you at death's door."

Mrs. Mohammed comes down the hall and stops right behind Zeina. I've met her before, at school and while out shopping, but never at her house.

"Come in," she says. Mrs. Mohammed's face looks so amazingly sad, even though she is trying to smile.

"Sure."

"No, I don't think so," Zeina snaps.

"I have asked Penelope to come into our home, so don't be rude. Plus, you have never had her over."

"I don't want her here."

Why? Is Zeina mad at me, too? It's a bleak, dreary, rainy day. The windows are up high at street level, so it would be dark anyway, and it's not like it would be easy for anybody to peek in, yet all the shades are drawn. And it smells funky. I gaze into the living room, and there on the couch is her dad, surrounded by piles of newspapers and clutter that is piled mountain-high. He's staring into space, and though I say, "Hi" just to be polite, he doesn't answer me.

So rude! Angry words rush to my lips but I clamp

down on them. I don't want to upset Zeina. I'll never, ever be invited back if I do.

My flashing eyes tell Zeina exactly what I'm thinking.

"Don't bother," she says. "He's not ignoring you. He is in one of those places now."

I don't know what to say or do. Mrs. Mohammed has put out milk and cookies and steers us into the kitchen. "I'm sorry, Penelope," she says. "When my husband is like this, he doesn't seem to hear what any of us are saying. Please don't take it personally."

"Why didn't you tell me?" I ask Zeina quietly.

"What, that my father is crazy?"

"He's not crazy, dear," says Mrs. Mohammed. Her voice is so soft, so gentle. I wish I had a mother with a voice like hers. "Zeina's father just got fired from his job as a waiter," she tells me.

"Fourth times in three months," Zeina adds, her voice a snarl.

"I thought he was a doctor?"

"In Syria. But when he came here, he was told he would have to redo his training, take all kinds of exams, and we need the money, so he waits tables. And gets fired. And gets angry," Zeina says, adding, "And this happens all the time!"

"This is often the life of immigrants in America," Mrs. Mohammed says. "He was a doctor. I was his nurse. And here I am a receptionist and he is a waiter who gets angry that people are giving him orders."

"Because he's *crazy*." Zeina is too furious to lower her voice, and I am scared that her father will hear and come roaring in to yell at us all.

"No, sweetheart. Because he's angry. Because he's

frustrated."

"You manage to keep your job, Mama."

"For the family!"

"What family?" Zeina turns to me. "Can you pretend that you didn't see any of this? We can talk about this some other time, I promise. Just not now!"

"Zeina!" Mrs. Mohammed is so annoyed.

"No worries, really!" I give Zeina a big hug. I can feel her bones, and I feel like weeping. Suddenly, I remember hugging my mom, and feeling her *LARGE* bones.

"Thanks, Mrs. Mohammed. I'm so sorry I stopped by at a bad time. I'll come back when it's a better time for a visit, okay?"

I walk out of the kitchen and head for the front door. I can't wait to get out of this awkward situation.

As I head home, I can't help wondering whether Zeina just joined the list of people who are not talking to me. Can I do anything right?

CHAPTER NINE

I come home from school tired, ready to veg.

"Eggplant parmesan for dinner." Dad is so perky it's maddening. "Are you okay?"

What should I say? Johnny said he doesn't care who I cast for Dad, as long as I can cast him in some part. Plus, he kissed me without my saying it was okay, which, according to him, makes *me* the jerk. No. No, no, no. I can't tell my dad that. Should I tell him that Zeina's dad, who is a doctor in Syria, sits around their home surrounded by years of newspapers in Arabic and English? Oh, and that he's lost his fourth job in three months as a waiter? Guess what else, Dad? None of my friends are talking to me, and I am now a social outcast. This is when I think I would prefer a mother; I assume a mother might be able to talk to me better. What should I tell Dad? That I'm okay?

"I'm fine," I say.

"Really?"

"Yeah."

"Then let's sit down and eat."

Too easy to get Dad to back off. "I'm not hungry."

"I made this really nice dinner for us."

"I had a late lunch."

I am too weirded out by my life to sit down and eat at the moment. I still can't get over how skinny Zeina is, Mr.

Mohammed, the kiss with Johnny, how I miss a mom I never knew. I feel bad for Dad, though.

"It smells good," I say. "Invite one of your friends over to eat with you."

Suddenly it occurs to me, Dad doesn't have any friends. There are some guys at work he sometimes goes out with, but for the most part, there is no one for him to talk to. All I have been saying to Dad recently is get a life, but this is it—his life.

Title for my next play: "Get a Life." Sucky title, not very original.

"It smells so good," I say, pulling out a chair. "I just have to try some."

Dad smiles broadly as he lifts a plate and cuts into the eggplant. "I think you'll love it. I used extra ricotta cheese, the way you like."

Sometimes in life you just have to eat the eggplant parmesan, even when you don't want to, because you love the person who made it.

A Heart Is Not Judged By How Much You Love; But By How Much You Are Loved By Others

The Wizard says this to Tin Man when he gives him his honorary heart. I'm not so sure it's true, but something I saw today made me think of it. I told you, I am writing a book about laundry called *Secrets of the Sheets*, and it is a book of poetry. I wrote this about a woman who takes in laundry at our local laundromat. The other day I was in there with my friend Ava whose locker is near mine. She was picking up her family's wash and asked if I could go with her. I figured I should go since Ava is one of the few friends I have who isn't angry at me at the moment.

The woman who works at the laundry was proudly showing everyone photos of her granddaughter who graduated college last May. She was telling how she had sent her through college with the money she had saved from her job there at the laundry. She inspired me to write this poem. I hope her granddaughter loves her back as much as she is loved by her grandmother.

OTHER PEOPLE'S LAUNDRY

For sixty-five years
She washed laundry—
dirty sheets,
knowing that
certain stains don't wash out.

Now—
stooped over,
her old joints
dance for joy,
so proud that the money she saved
helped a girl
like she once was,
go to college
so she could wash
only her own sheets.

CHAPTER TEN

If I were writing a story, I would call this "A Day with the Rents." That's what I call my grandparents because it's what Dad calls them. *What came first, the chicken or the egg?*—Dad plays this whenever we are walking the three blocks from the subway station to the attached three-story house where my grandparents live.

"It has to be the chicken. Otherwise who could have laid the egg?" But the chicken had to be born from the egg, didn't it? It makes my head hurt just to think about it.

"What came first—our visit to your grandparents—or me?"

"Dad, obviously *you* came first—or there would be no visiting the rents!"

"No. The other way around. They loved me, so they wanted me to arrive."

Now I know he is really losing it. I also know, despite our delay in seeing them, we are clearly off to see the rents. Why does Dad call them the rents? Because they help him with the rent—at least, at one time they did. For as long as I remember, they took care of me—stayed with me during the day when I was little, picked me up from school when I got older. I suddenly get it—par-*rents*! Amusing, I guess.

"Does seeing Grandma and Zayde make you nervous?" I ask as we walk up the steps to their house.

"No," he says. "Why should it?"

"Don't ask me," I say. "They're your parents. And you always seem nervous before we get to their house."

"Well...I'm not nervous," he says, ringing the front doorbell. "It might be because they ask so many questions. Plus, they have so many opinions about how I should live my life."

"So, the answer is yes. They make you nervous," I say.

Grandma is old and it takes her a while to answer the front doorbell. We know this so we settle in to wait. I lean on the wrought iron rail and look around. Down on the sidewalk a woman passes us pushing twin babies in a wide stroller. She wears a blond wig that's not even on straight. My grandparents live in another part of Brooklyn—Borough Park—where men and women covered in dark clothes walk to *shul* and pray, mostly the men. They are called Orthodox Jews. The women stay home and cook and raise the kids. Grandma says it doesn't mean women aren't important in the home; the women rule, as Grandma likes to say. In the Orthodox temple where Zayde prays, I'm sometimes allowed to sit with him, even though the men and women are separated. Zayde rocks to and fro when he prays; it's sweet and comforting. He mostly prays for my dad to find a wife; at least this is what he tells me, even though it doesn't look like it will happen any time soon.

I once asked Grandma why some of the women around her neighborhood wear awful wigs that no one would ever mistake for real hair.

"It's a way of covering their hair, like a hat or a scarf. Only married women are required to do it."

"Is that why you wear a scarf?" I asked her.

"Yes."

"My Muslim friend, Zeina, wears a headscarf. Obviously, she's not married."

Grandma shrugged her shoulders. "Different strokes for different folks," she said with a smile.

Now, after seeing all the women in bad wigs, scarves, and hats on the streets, I'm thinking about headscarves, hats, and wigs. Does that kind of modesty keep boys from pressing up against you and kissing you without permission? Maybe I should think about wearing a wig or a scarf. Nah, Johnny would have just asked what was up with the wig and then kissed me anyway.

Grandma appears, beaming, overjoyed to see us. She lets us in and I kiss her cheek.

"Eat, *sheina meidala*," she says before I even take off my coat.

"I can't eat, Grandma. It's eleven in the morning."

The thought of matzo balls that fall to the bottom of my stomach like bombs is sickening! She gives me those sad eyes.

"I just had breakfast," I tell her. I can imagine what she would say if she saw Zeina.

"For me," Zayde appeals.

Zayde is Solomon the Wise, the loving grandpa who read me adult books when I was little. The author Dostoevsky is his favorite. Though I didn't understand the words, I loved their sound. I have to eat for Zayde because I adore him.

"My writer," Zayde says as I scoop the soup into my mouth. "I want you to write my story."

"Grandpa, I have so many stories to write."

"So mine will be one more!" He pauses, eyes bright,

struck with a new thought. "Can you show me how to use my new phone?"

"No problem," I tell Zayde.

"I just learned how to use the last one and then I dropped it in a puddle and now I have to learn a whole other thing. These phone companies want you to always have to buy the next big product."

"I'm sure they've upgraded the operating system since your last phone," I say.

"Upped the what?"

I smile. "Don't worry. I'll show you after supper. It's probably the same as the phone I have."

"Kalman," Grandma says abruptly.

"Charles, Ma. I told you to call me Charles."

Maybe my Dad and I are not so different after all! They do not call me Pilar; they call me Fagye, my Jewish name, and they are probably the only people I do not bother to correct.

"What about looking for a wife, a mother for Fagye?"

"Ma, haven't we discussed this a million times too many?"

Zayde chimes in, "She means well," as Grandma plops this orange monstrosity called pot roast in front of me, and now the arguments begin between the wolf, my dad, and the bull, my grandma.

Zayde begs them to stop, but not before Grandma tells me I need to continue practicing my Torah portion; it is only a month away.

"I am," I lie, half choking on the matzo ball I am having enormous trouble swallowing.

"Kalman," Grandma says. "Don't you think our Fagye is starting to look like Rhoda Morgenstern?"

"Who?" Dad and I ask at the same time.

"The girl who was the friend of Mary Richards on TV," Grandma says.

"Do you mean on *The Mary Tyler Moore Show*?" Dad asks. Grandma nods.

I'm already Googling Rhoda Morgenstern. Wikipedia says that in 1970 an actress named Valerie Harper first played a character named Rhoda Morgenstern. The first thing I notice is that she's very pretty, so I hope Grandma is right and not just losing her eyesight. The second thing, though, is that she wears all these super cute headscarves. In every photo she has a different one wrapped around her forehead with the ends of the scarf trailing down.

I show Grandma the picture on my screen. "Yes, that's her," Grandma says. "I always loved how she wore those scarves."

"Me, too!" I cry. "How would I look in a scarf tied like that?"

Grandma goes to her bedroom and returns with a purple scarf. She fashions it around my head, Rhoda Morgenstern style. "It suits you," she says.

I check it out in the front hall mirror and smile. It definitely suits me.

CHAPTER ELEVEN

I'm supposed to have dinner with Zeina, though I'm not in the mood. Grandma is right; I should practice my Torah portion, so I don't embarrass myself in front of everyone. I should also try to finish my play, since I told Ms. Reise I would—maybe. I feel kind of lazy, but then remind myself I have a whole day off tomorrow—three-day Veteran's Day weekend. I promised Mrs. Mohammed I would work on our school social studies project with Zeina at her house, since Zeina's mom doesn't want people staying away from the house because of her dad. So, I go. Zeina's been deranged about this, but hey, aren't we all deranged about something?

"Hi," I say when I arrive, ignoring the grimace on Zeina's face and the fact that she is despondent. Zeina's family lives in an apartment halfway below street level; I can see people's feet passing by on the sidewalk outside her windows. That is, I *could*, except that today all the shades are once again pulled closed; there is not one ounce of light in the room. I would go nuts if I had to live in the dark like this.

"What's your story?" I ask, annoyed at the gloom and her sulking.

"Nothing. What's yours? You know I don't like to work here."

"Your mother wanted me to."

"If my mother wanted you to jump off the Brooklyn Bridge, would you?"

"You don't have to be so snarky—not to mention trite and clichéd."

"I do have to because nothing else gets through to you," Zeina replies, "and besides it's not trite to use a traditional American saying."

"Is so."

"Not!"

I can tell this is going to be a *great* day.

While we work, Zeina only talks about our project on the building of the transcontinental railroad. "They were so awful to the Chinese," I say. "So unfair."

Zeina lifts her head, about to speak, but decides against it.

"Don't you think so?" I press her.

"Mm-hmm," she says with a nod.

"I have to go to the bathroom," I say.

"Then go," she snaps, so I do.

After I'm finished washing my hands, I go out into the tiny hallway and peek into the shadowy living room. I decide to say "Hi" to Mr. Mohammed again, since Dad has said I shouldn't treat him like he's crazy. It is clear Zeina doesn't want to introduce me to her dad, so it's on me to introduce myself. I go into the living room, where the television is on, but it is blurry; there's no picture.

"Hi, Mr. Mohammed," I say, and he looks at me with a blank stare. "I'm Penny, Zeina's friend," I say again. There's no sense getting into the whole Pilar thing, since Mrs. Mohammed already calls me Penny.

"Penny. We've never formally met." Mr. Mohammed

takes my hand, holds it, fleetingly and then drops it, not knowing what to do with it. He opens his mouth, then closes it, as that crazed look returns to his eyes.

"What are you doing?" asks Zeina, standing in the doorway.

"I am trying to introduce myself to your dad. Last time I was here, you didn't bother."

"You can forget that. He is in his no-speech mode." Zeina glares at her father and then shifts her angry eyes toward me.

Mrs. Mohammed comes out of the kitchen. "Zeina, calm down. Penny did nothing wrong."

Wrong? What could I have done that was wrong? Now I am flipping out, furious at Zeina. Not sure what to do with my anger. Should I exit the house, or apologize to Zeina—for what, I am not sure. Maybe she's right. Her Dad seems crazy—the way he touched my hand and stared. It really seemed kind of scary. I follow Zeina, who has stomped off to her room. Once we are inside, she slams the door and whirls on me.

"Why did you do that?"

"Do what?"

"Go into the living room."

"I just wanted to talk to your dad!"

"You know he's off. Isn't that enough for you? Did you ever stop to think about why I wouldn't introduce you?"

Not really, I think. If my mother were alive, even if she were crazy, she would still be my mother. Zeina has too many secrets. Friends are supposed to open up, to share, and to get rid of secrets.

"Now you know," she stammers. "It's worse than I told you."

She starts crying and pounding the bed. I am petrified. Zeina is always so calm, so reserved.

"I'm sorry you felt you couldn't share this with me, Zeina." Oh, my God, I sound like Reise.

"I told you last time. Isn't that enough for you, Penny? Isn't anything enough?"

"I'm your closest friend. It's what friends do. Tell me, Zeina. I'm not going to judge you!"

I've never seen Zeina this way. Her slumped body lies face-down on the bed, panting heavily into her pillow, reminding me of a defeated, captured animal. Gradually, she sits up and her next words tumble passionately from her lips.

"Ever since we left Syria where Dad was a doctor and he's had to make money working as a waiter, which he hates, he's been off. But you knew this. You knew Mom was a nurse, and now she's not certified to work at her real job, either. You knew my father didn't want me to come to your bat mitzvah. Isn't that enough? Mom, who was my father's nurse, is now a health aide, cleaning other people's shit from bedpans. Dad loses it on customers *all the time*—and then he gets fired–and then he goes wild. I told you, stomping around the house, watching the blank television screen. And he's gone now, lost somewhere in his head, and it can be months before he comes back again."

Zeina's soft, pretty face is practically unrecognizable now—a mass of tears and snot. Her long eyelashes, which I've always secretly wished I had, are sticking together in soggy points. And this is where words fail me; what can I say now that would make it any better? Is nothing ever enough for me? How do I always manage to make things worse when I'm trying so hard to make them better?

I hug her. I hold her. I whisper, "I'm sorry."

And I know that is really pretty lame. But "sorry" is all I have to give her. What is wrong with me? Why can't I be a good friend to Zeina?

"Is that why you don't eat?"

"Sometimes."

Some writer I've turned out to be–a writer who never has the right words when she needs them.

CHAPTER TWELVE

Today I *must* practice my Torah portion. Mostly, I really think I have to pray. I'm doing this for my Zayde, because it means so much to him. I'm doing this for all his family who died in the Holocaust, and Grandma's family, too. I practice the Friday night candle-lighting ceremony prayer. *Baruch atah Adonai, Eleheinu, melech haolam, asher, kid'shanu b'mitzvotav, v'tzivanu, l'hadlik ner shel Shabbat.*

I'm practicing. I told Grandma that I would practice, so I'm doing this for her, too. I am doing this for all the ghosts she has on her walls. *Baruch atah, Adonai, Eloheinu, melech haolam, asher kid'shanu b'mitzvotav, v'tzivanu, l'hadlik ner shel Shabbat.*

I'm doing this for my father because he wants to please his parents because then they'll be off his case, especially Grandma. *Baruch atah, Adonai, Eloheinu, melech Haolam, asher kid'shanu b'mitzvotav, v'tzivanu I'hadlik ner shel Shabbat.*

I am doing this for Zeina. Isn't that crazy? I'm praying for her dad since if Mr. Mohammed is happier, perhaps Zeina won't be so sad, and keep it all buried. *Baruch atah, Adonai, Eloheinu, melech Haolam, asher, kid'shanu b'mitzvotav, v'tzivanu, I'hadlik ner shel Shabbat.*

I practice my Torah portion, too, one time, two times,

twenty, forty, fifty times. More than just this simple blessing for the candle-lighting.

I am doing this for everyone, except for me. I want to learn to be unselfish.

CHAPTER THIRTEEN

Lazy day in bed—a little television, some homework; plus, Dad is out of the house all day. He's visiting his brother, Herbie, on Long Island. He wanted me to go with him, but I knew that would mean day and night; Herbie and Dad usually like to go out to dinner. Now I know I'll be asleep by the time he gets home. Yes! Yes! Yes!

Grandma gave me her purple scarf. It takes me a few tries before I can tie it in the Rhoda Morgenstern style. Finally, I get it right. I really love the way I look. I take a selfie and caption it "TRYING A NEW LOOK." I'm about to post it on Instagram, but I change my mind. I don't want to see the snarky comments that could come my way. Why open myself up to that? I leave the picture on my phone. I might post it when I'm feeling friendlier toward the world.

I wish I felt like I could hit up Zeina, ask her to hang out at the library or something. That's how we met—we kept seeing each other at the library, and finally one of us, I don't even remember who, said, "What are you reading?" It was probably me who said it, because Zeina was too shy to talk to anybody right after she got here, even though her English was already pretty good. It turned out we liked all the same books. At first, I was the one recommending things—*Harriet the Spy, From the Mixed-Up Files of Mrs. Basil E. Frankweiler, A Tree Grows in Brooklyn* and other stuff she didn't know about in America. Soon, Zeina was telling me about books like *Stargazer* and *Turtles All the Way Down*. When the poet who wrote *Brown Girl Dreaming* gave a reading at the Barnes & Noble last year, we both went and got our copies autographed. It was amazing to be in the same room with the woman who wrote those poems, hearing her speak out loud the words I've heard so many times in my own head as I've read her book. Listening to her—a Brooklyn girl born in Ohio, who grew up and became a Brooklyn woman and a Brooklyn writer—was one of the first times I understood that I, a plain, ordinary person living in Brooklyn, could write my own story and people might actually want to read it.

But now I'm bored. I'm also starved. There's nothing to eat in the house. Plus, I've deposited the last of my babysitting money in the bank. My father has secret hiding places for cash. Tomorrow I'll tell him I borrowed some of it. I've told little white lies, but I would never lie big time to Dad.

I search and I search. Every hidden drawer and nook and cranny. Finally, at the bottom of the drawer—a hidden stash—$20.00. Good, I can get Chinese food. I'm sick of pizza.

But there's something else—a diary. It actually says DIARY. I can't imagine Dad keeping a diary, but who knows? Curiosity gets the best of me.

Oh, my God, oh, my God, oh, my God—the Diary of Star Lasky? My mother? Why did he keep this? Was he saving it for me—a token, a memory of who she was before she died. I can't wait. This is just so crazy. I can't figure it out. I feel like I have found Anne Frank. My own Anne Frank, right in my own family, and she is my mother.

And I have hours and hours to read it before my Dad gets home.

****

This diary is dense. Forty pages. She skips around; it is all over the place. I am all over the place; I am reeling, but I *want* people to understand what is happening to me now, since I do not know what is happening, aside from the fact that I am so deeply disturbed. I can't write everything. I can't share everything. My insides are doing somersaults. So, this is not the full diary; this is just bits and pieces.

CHAPTER FOURTEEN

THE DIARY OF STAVAN/STAR LASKY

I can't put down my mother's diary. I lie across my bed, my head held in one hand, the diary in front of me, shifting only occasionally to reposition myself as my arm or leg needs a stretch. If my room were on fire I wonder if I would even notice. That's how wrapped up I am in what my mother has written.

Her words are not always easy to follow. Her thinking is disjointed and chaotic. Most confusing is the fact that sometimes she refers to herself as Stavan, and then she becomes Star. Then, out of nowhere, she talks about Mr. Lasky. It seems as if she is not referring to Dad, but to herself. *What? She is three people?* The things she is writing are so weird; I am not sure I understand them. But I keep reading.

*

My soul floats out of my body. It's a man's soul in a woman's body. No one ever lets me be a man. I love Charles, but I am the one who wears the pants, who abhors cooking and cleaning, who loves plumbing, woodworking, wearing men's clothes. Could I, Star, marry a woman and be a man? My brothers and sisters tell me no. But Charles is the woman I have dreamed of—cooking, cleaning, singing show tunes in the kitchen. He could be the wife. And I could be the husband.

*

My mother tells me, "No, no, you have a great fiancé. Do not blow it, Star. He will buy you a diamond ring. Keep that man thing a secret. Zip it up. The diamond will glitter on your finger."

*

Actually, I want to be a bride. A bride, a man, or a writer. I want to wear a long, white veil—fifty feet long. Attack of the Fifty Foot Woman.

*

What is she talking about? Why is she bringing up a horror film? This just does not make sense. It seems from the parts I am reading that she did not love my Dad. Or she wanted to be married—but maybe not to a man.

*

And when I am a bride, I will have the most gorgeous white gown with pearl buttons adorning every inch of it. The buttons will be like eyes. They will see right through me.

*

When I am that bride, I will be like a Queen. I will be Queen Elizabeth, married to Prince Philip...no, Prince Charles. My prince is named Charles. I will order my servants around. Charles will be my servant. He likes when I giggle. He does not like it when I roar. I can be a lion, but I can also be a lamb. "Roll of thunder, hear me roar."

*

My mother made me go to secretarial school. I asked her why I couldn't go to carpentry school or plumbing school, and she insisted it was not for a girl, even though I had always fixed all the appliances in the house. I did not want to be a secretary, but I pretended.

*

God is dead; God is dead; God is dead. Sometimes I scream this in the house when no one is around.

*

Why is she screaming 'God is dead'? What is wrong with her? What does God have to do with it? Is there a God?

*

Yes, I would rather be a king on a royal throne. King Solomon, the Wise, like Charles' father. I don't have to wear stupid dresses; I hate them. I only like them when I decide I want to be a Princess. I can wear pants all the time. I can demand everyone does what I want them to do when I want them to do it.

*

I always knew I was different growing up. I had very few friends. I mostly liked to stay in my room and write— reams and reams of paper. I even wrote on napkins, on toilet paper. So many stories bursting through the seams.

*

Oh, my God; oh, my God! I am suffocating; I can't breathe. This is why I write. My mother did, too. She wanted to be a writer. Or a plumber. Or a carpenter. Or a king. Or my father. Not sure I can continue reading this, but I have to! I wonder how she felt being a mother. Not sure I want to know. Not certain I want to get to know her any better, yet I have to move forward. The entries are random, chaotic, like her mind must have been. I don't know how much time is passing. Right now, I am feeling random, chaotic, scared.

*

Everyone is whispering about me. Everywhere I go. They are saying that I'm bad. I hear them in my head. Whispering! Whispering! Always whispering about me!

*

The wedding was a splendid affair. I had trouble finding a maid of honor, since I have very few female friends. I asked Lacy, Charles' sister, even though I don't think she likes me.

*

Aunt Lacy didn't like my mother? This is so hard to believe. She likes everyone! This is crazy. I love my Aunt Lacy; I love her children, Deirdre and Robert. Maybe she thought my mother was not well.

*

Maybe Charles can have the baby he is dying for. All he ever talks about is that he wants children. Well, let him have them!

*

Now I am pregnant. I'm scared of this baby, since lately I am hearing more and more voices. The voices tell me to get rid of the baby. They yell at me and I yell right back!

*

My mother didn't want me. She never wanted a baby? I want to shout. I want to scream. I want to rip this diary to shreds.

*

Charles tells me to quit my job, so I do, since it is too much of a woman's job, and you know how I feel about that. He says I should relax more that maybe that will make the voices stop. What I don't tell him is that I like the voices; they are my friends!

*

I am feeling my pulse for the first time. What if I jam my fingers up against it? What if I mangle my veins? What if I kill this baby?

*

Did she really want to kill me?

*

I will love this baby so much that I will want her to stay inside me forever.
She is born and she is beautiful.
I love her; she is the sun, moon, stars, and earth.

*

She loves me. At least she says she loves me. And that I was born beautiful!

*

Penelope Lasky, named after my dearly departed

father, Philip. Big blue eyes. Wisps of blonde hair on her head.

*

She is so tiny and stunning, so sweet I could suffocate her.

*

They say I can feed her with my body, but I can barely feed myself.

Charles tells me he is sorry. That he made a phone call. He keeps saying he is sorry, that I left him no choice. The men in white coats are going to come to take me away. Lacy will come to stay with Charles, and bring her daughter, Deirdre. I hate him, but I am too tired to move.

*

Where will they take her? She is my mama. I don't recall any of this.

*

My baby. My baby. My baby. Bring me home to my baby.

*

I love Penelope more than I love myself. It is not a mother's love; it is a father's. When I come home, the voices are gone. They gave me medicine to make them go away, but I miss them. I cook; I clean; I take care of Penny. It is the me I want to be, but not really.

*

I do this for months. I mother my sheina meidala. I love her like no other. And the days and weeks and months go by. I forget to write.

*

Suddenly, she is two, in the blink of an eye. It is winter. I miss the warmth. I dress like a man since the voices—which have returned—say I can be whatever I want to be. I do not tell Charles my voices are back, because he will make me go away again if he knows. It is so terribly cold outside, and Penny loves to play in the snow. I hate, hate, hate, winter. The voices tell me to kill her so I don't have to take her out in the snow. But I'm her mother, so I dress her warmly and hurry her out the door in case I start to believe the voices. Outside she'll be safe from me. I must keep her safe from me. I'm her mother and her father.

*

Now I am alone. It's quieter without the child. I start writing again. My words are like knives. They are my weapon. They are my protection.

If words are knives, then I can kill you with them if I want. Who shall I kill?

*

Charles is home and he is screaming, ranting like a lunatic. He says how dare I.

"How dare I do what?"

"Leave a toddler outside alone."

"It was better for her out there."

I can barely finish as his voice rises and rises. He shoves me to the ground, throws things. Crouched on the floor, I explain that it was better to lock her out of the apartment than to kill her.

"Kill her?!" he shouts. "Kill her?!" His eyes bulge. His face reddens.

"The voices told me to kill her, so I locked her out for her own safety," I repeat.

That is just logical. But he can't see it that way. He is raging around the room as though he is the one who is insane. He certainly appears to have lost his mind.

*

If he is the one who has gone insane, then why, dear God, are there men here who are trying to drag me out of my apartment? Luckily my bedroom door locks, and I have run inside to escape them. Outside, in the hall, the white-coated men murmur as they whisper and plot against me. They knock. "Come on, Mrs. Lasky, come out now. We're not here to hurt you." Liars! Will they come in the window? Will they knock the door down? They want to take me away from my precious child who I only want to love, who I cherish more than life itself. I can't stay in here! I will leave this room to fight them with the strength of ten men—

to fight with all the fierceness within my heart! I will die before I let them take me! Here I go!

CHAPTER FIFTEEN

I clutch my phone and can't stop crying.

Zeina's voice shouts at me from the other end. "What are you saying?"

More crying. More sobbing.

"Cut it out," says Zeina. "I'm not mad at you anymore. Forget about it!"

"It's not about us, Zeina. It's about my mother."

"Your mother? What about her? I thought she died ages ago, when you were just a baby. Why are you crying so hard about her now?"

"I think she may be alive."

Zeina says something, but I miss it, because I can't stop crying. "Wh—what?"

"I said, 'What are you talking about?'" I can almost picture Zeina, tapping her foot to maintain patience.

"See, you're not the only one with secrets."

I sniffle a huge glob of snot back up into my nose. The sound is disgusting; I hope Zeina won't call me out on it.

"I know this sounds crazy, but I found my mother's diary."

"I can hardly hear you." Zeina is beyond exasperated

"My mother kept a diary, Zeina. She wanted to be a man. She heard voices in her head. She didn't want to get pregnant, but then she did. Then I was born, but then she didn't want me, either, and there are all these blank pages and confused thoughts. It's so scary. There were accusations that my dad said she was a terrible mother and she did things like lock me out of the house in the snow and she said she wanted to kill me. And the next thing you know, she's taken away. She's gone."

"Okay, that's really terrible. No wonder you're so upset!" Zeina pauses to think about it. "Look, I don't know how to say this without upsetting you even worse, so–try to be calm, all right? The thing is–how do you know she's still alive? What makes you think so?"

"I *don't* know. That's one of the things that's so bad! I only know Dad lied when he told me she died when I was little. If he lied about that, I can't believe anything he says, can I?"

Zeina hesitates. "Maybe she died. Maybe she killed herself."

"I don't believe it, but now I want to kill my dad, I'm so mad at him!"

"You need to talk to him. Maybe after the awards ceremony tomorrow."

"No kidding, I need to talk to him! But as far as the awards ceremony, now I am really not going."

"You have to go. You're getting an award."

"For an unfinished play based on a big bunch of lies, told to me by my big fat liar of a dad–a play which surely will never be finished now."

"Come on, Pilar. You're a writer. It's nice that the school is acknowledging that."

"My mother was a writer, too, and a lot of good it did her. I need to know what happened to her, where she is!"

"All I am saying is wait. Wait till after the ceremony.

Just be quiet, get your award, stay cool and wait a day or two. This way you can cool off."

"I'm not going to cool off!"

"Oh, c'mon." Zeina sounds so reasonable that I almost hate her, too. "Things will get better."

"Really. Has it gotten any better for you with your Dad?" This is mean, and I know it.

She sighs. "No. Not really. But I can pretend if I have to, and so can you."

She sounds so sad, and all of a sudden I am ashamed of myself for yelling at my best friend, whose only crime is trying to be helpful. I give in.

"Okay, I suppose that makes sense. I guess I can, just for you. One thing you gotta promise me, though. No more secrets between us—ever?"

I can hear the smile on her face. "Yeah! Sounds like a plan!"

I can't tell if Zeina feels as upbeat as she sounds. It doesn't matter. I'm lucky she's my friend.

But once we hang up, I'm alone-more alone than I've ever been in my life. I crouch like an infant in fetal position, feeling so sad that I don't know what to do with it. I sob silently, wondering about my mother, if she's alive—I think she is!—and if she ever loved me. Then why was it so easy for her to leave? Why didn't she come back and try to love me?

CHAPTER SIXTEEN

I suck at making happy faces. The whole day at school, all I can think about is my mother and my father. Why did he lie to me? When did he become such a good actor? Zeina is right; I have to stop thinking about this till after the awards ceremony.

"Ready?" Dad stands at the door, a bouquet of roses in his hand, red and yellow, my favorite colors.

"For me?"

"For my writer." He is beaming ear to ear, a goofy smile pasted across his face.

He's dressed casually, trying to look relaxed, something he never is—khaki pants, loose, long-sleeved shirt, loafers. I am used to seeing him in work attire: a tie, polished Oxfords, and all-around fancier than the other engineers in his firm look. He still looks stiff and uncomfortable. The only time I see him looking different is when he's at the stove singing his goofy Broadway tunes. This is when I like Dad the best. But now I am too mad to like him. He lied to me.

"Ready, spaghetti?"

"As ready as ever."

I talk to myself. Do not forget what Zeina said. This can wait till tomorrow, or even the next day. She said this would allow me to cool off, though I feel all hot around the ears.

We walk to school, barely talking, barely touching.

"Everything okay?"

"Fine," I lie.

"There's a surprise for you tonight!"

Surprise. What's a bigger surprise than the diary? I don't want your stupid surprise. I want my mother. Give her back to me, Dad. Give her back this minute. She wasn't yours to take away.

I hope she is still alive. My mother may be dead, or else she may be in some terrible place, sitting, waiting for me, doing nothing. I have to stop thinking about this. I have to answer Dad.

"Really?"

"Oh, yes." He looks so pleased with himself that I want to scream.

We get to the school and head to the auditorium. While we are looking for two seats reasonably close to the aisle—so I can march up to the stage and collect my meaningless award when the time comes—I notice Johnny making some weird hand signals at me. I shrug my shoulders, like I have no idea what he is trying to say to me, and mouth, "I have no idea what you are saying." It's bothering me, though, because this is the first time Johnny has really tried to talk to me since that awkward kiss we both can't wait to forget about. It's been "Yes" and "No" and "Right," and that's about it. While I'm glad Johnny's talking to me again, I'm pretty uneasy because it's obviously important, otherwise he wouldn't be carrying on like a mime with Tourette's.

It's like he's trying to warn me about something, but I wish he wouldn't. I don't need to feel anything is any more dangerous than it already is. An ominous cloud hangs in the air, and I feel like I am trapped in toxic smog. I really don't care about this stupid award. In order to calm down and keep my mind off everything, I compose a blog while I am waiting, tapping it into my phone:

Over the Rainbow, Blog #11: This award is a charade. I don't know what I feel. I also don't know what I am. The play is not finished, so why am I getting this lame award anyway?

I am in the middle of trying to come up with an appropriate title for my vent from *The Wizard of Oz*, when I hear, "And before we honor eighth grader Penelope Lasky, with the Budding Writer Award, we have a small scene to share with you."

I whip around. "What scene?" I ask my Dad.

"From your unfinished play." He smiles happily.

"Pardon me?" I snap.

"Ms. Reise begged me, and I said I knew you'd be thrilled!"

I look up at the stage, and there are my alleged friends Ava and Calvin, playing me and Dad, respectively. I suspect Johnny turned down the role of the Dad, since he knew how I felt. This is what all the hand flapping was about.

I let it sink in. Sink into me like a knife.

"I didn't give Reise permission," I hiss in a high-pitched whisper.

"I did." The heat in my head turns instantly to ice. The words from the diary start thumping away in my head. *How dare he how dare he how dare he.*

This can't be real.

"*You* did!? It isn't yours!" I say. "You had no right to give permission."

"I thought you'd be happy afterward."

"It's not your play!" My heart races. "*Not-your-play!*"

I start trembling uncontrollably. I'm ready to run but instead I slide from my chair onto my knees. The room spins. There's an outraged creature in my head, clawing its way out. It's wild to escape! I have to let it out! I fall backward, banging my head against the floor. *Slam!*

The creature in my head keeps me pinned there. It is banging its way out of my head, fueled by fire and rage. It bangs and bangs, frantic to escape. I have to keep on banging, though I can feel people trying to pull me away from the floor. I open my mouth to scream, but nothing comes out. It is stuck inside.

And now I understand, I am really:

Crazy!

Crazy!

Crazy!

Crazy!

CONFIDENTIAL PSYCHOLOGICAL EVALUATION

IDENTIFYING INFORMATION

Name: Penelope Lasky, A.K.A. Pilar
Gender: Female
Date of Birth: 09/14/2006
Ethnicity: Jewish-American
Age: 13 years, 3 months
Education: 9 years
Occupation: Student
Date(s) of Examination: 12/6/2019 and 12/10/2019
Parent/Guardian: Charles Lasky
Examiner: Joan Shoane, PhD

TESTS/PROCEDURES ADMINISTERED   DATE

Clinical Interview	**12/6/2019**
Parent Questionnaire	**12/6/2019**
Talking Map	**12/10/2019**
Stages of Confident Speaking	**12/10/2019**
MRI, CT Scan	

REASON FOR REFERRAL

Miss Lasky is a 13-year-old, right-handed, Jewish-American female, who was referred to Joan Shoane, Ph.D. after being discharged from the Psychiatry Department at Brookville University Hospital Medical Center on 12/10/2019. The examiner reviewed the limits of confidentiality and obtained a signed informed consent form from the patient's parent/guardian. Miss Lasky agreed to participate in the testing process but refuses to speak. The therapist will discuss feedback and treatment plan with parent and child during next appointment on 12/17/2019.

PRESENTING COMPLAINTS

Mr. Lasky describes his daughter as a generally well-adjusted adolescent but reports a recent change in mood due to an incident that occurred at school in December. Mr. Lasky believes a recent incident at school may have caused his daughter to stop speaking. Mr. Lasky states that his daughter is uncomfortable sharing her writing and recently won an award. Mr. Lasky gave permission for writing to be performed as a play. Miss Lasky was overcome with stress upon seeing her play performed and responded to her stress and anxiety through means of self-harm: head-banging. Miss Lasky was taken to hospital due to self-harming behaviors and was discharged 24 hours later once it was determined she was not continuing to self-harm. During discussion Miss Lasky portrays signs of discomfort and stress as evidenced by the therapist through her different facial expressions. Miss Lasky responds through small gestures and facial expressions but continues to lack the ability to speak. Miss Lasky has a past diagnosis of selective mutism at the age of three.

BACKGROUND HISTORY

Medical History

Miss Lasky's medical history is significant for allergies (citrus, dust, strawberries). No serious physical injuries, surgeries, or physical illnesses were ever reported. Miss Lasky does not wear glasses. Hearing is within the normal limits. She indicates through a head nod that her appetite and sleep habits are fine. She reports sleeping between six and seven hours per night by means of a number chart she was willing to point to when asked.

Miss Lasky suffered from childhood selective mutism and did attend therapy sessions at the age of three. Mr. Lasky states that her mother had "left their lives" around this time. It was observed that Miss Lasky began to show signs of tearfulness when her mother was mentioned. Miss Lasky has not been engaged in therapy since the age of four. Miss Lasky was not willing to engage in guided discussion after mother was discussed.

Miss Lasky does not take any prescribed medications.

Family Medical and Psychiatric History

Miss Lasky's family history is remarkable for breast cancer (father's side of the family). Mr. Lasky disclosed to therapist after session that the mother suffers from schizophrenia and resides in a residential facility. Mr. Lasky indicated Miss Lasky is not aware of mother's past or current psychiatric history. Mr. Lasky states, "It is in

Pilar's best interest to not be told about her mother."

Miss Lasky writes on a notepad given to her, "My family does not believe in mental illness. We are all crazy anyway." This statement is important to note when taking in future cultural considerations.

Substance Use/Abuse History

Miss Lasky reports she currently does not drink alcohol or use any substances by shaking her head back and forth. Mr. Lasky states he drinks about one glass of wine per day. He states that this has not affected his family's lifestyle.

Developmental, Family, and Social History

Miss Lasky was born in Brooklyn, New York and her primary language is English. All developmental milestones are within normal limits. Speech before presentation of psychosocial stress at age of three was developmentally appropriate. Speech improved drastically after selective mutism diagnosis at age three and therapy from age three to four. Selective mutism at that time attributed to a traumatic event: the loss of mother from the home.

Mr. Lasky reports no concerns with speech from the age of four until recent hospitalization.

According to Miss Lasky's father, she aspires to take a job working as a writer after attending a university someday. Miss Lasky is an only child. Her immediate family is not in contact with her mother's family. Her immediate family consists of herself and her father. Miss Lasky is close with paternal grandparents. No romantic interests were reported with either parent or client. Therapist is only aware of Miss Lasky being interested in writing. Miss Lasky often shrugged her shoulders and looked out the window. Mr. Lasky describes her strengths as being a hard worker and a good listener. He states her weakness is that she has a temper and is occasionally angry.

December 12, 2019

Joan Shoane, PhD

Treatment Plan

Recipient Information	Provider Information
Medicaid Number: 12345678	Medicaid Provider Number: 937234567
Name: Penelope Lasky	Name: Joan Shoane, PhD
DOB: 09/14/2006	Treatment Plan Date: 12/12/2019
Other Agencies Involved:	**Plan to Coordinate Services:**
(Name of school)	Request teacher to complete Achenbach Teacher Report Form (TRF) 1 time during the first month of treatment. Continued contact by phone as needed.

Problem/Symptom: Selective/Traumatic Mutism as manifested by consistent failure to speak not due to lack of intelligence or being uncomfortable with the English language.

Long Term Goal: Symptoms will be significantly reduced and will no longer interfere with Penelope's functioning. This will be measured by Talking Map and Stages of Confident Speaking questionnaire during last session.

Anticipated completion date: Sometime in spring

Short Term Goals/ Objectives:	Date Established	Projected Completion Date	Date Achieved
1. Determine what stage of communication the client is in various settings	12/12/19	1/12/20	
2. Increase confidence and self-esteem significantly in order to allow client to gain control in situation	12/12/19	3/12/20	
3. Lower anxiety by utilizing breathing	12/12/19	2/20/20	

techniques, muscle relaxation, etc.		
4. Move from nonverbal to verbal ability to engage	12/12/19	4/2/20
5. Help client access feelings and emotions	12/12/19	Ongoing

Intervention/Action:	Responsible Person:
Individual therapy to help Penelope learn and implement coping skills for anxiety and help identify, process, and resolve feelings and emotions in order to move from nonverbal to verbal in all environments of daily life.	Joan Shoane, PhD
	What is going on? Why are they talking like this? I was in the emergency room? I can still read. I read what they write. I will not fill in the left part of this chart. Left is bad luck. My grandma

<table>
<tr><td></td><td>told me that.</td></tr>
<tr><td></td><td>P.L.</td></tr>
</table>

Comprehensive Psychiatric Emergency Room (CPEP) at
Brookville Medical Center
Brooklyn, NY 11212
(718) 240-5205

DISCHARGE SUMMARY
Date of Admission:12/6/2019
Date of Exam: 12/21/2019
Time of Exam: 7:14:10 PM
Patient Name: Penelope Lasky
Patient Number: 10020105441

This discharge summary consists of
1. The Initial Assessment,
2. Clinician's Narrative, and
3. Discharge Status and Instructions

---

1.   INITIAL PSYCHIATRIC ASSESSMENT

Complete Evaluation

Penelope is a 13-year-old Jewish American. She is
unwilling to speak to staff, but will communicate by

writing on notepad. Her chief complaint is unhappiness and psychological pain. She states she was "overcome with stress at school" and utilized self-harm (head banging) as a means for coping. Client presents as anxious and tearful.

Her symptoms include:
    Sleep Disturbance
    Irritability
    Difficulty concentrating or mind going blank
    Being easily fatigued
    Based on the risk of morbidity without treatment and Penelope's description of interference with functioning, severity is estimated to be moderate.

Penelope has had no prior episodes of self-harm.

Problem Pertinent Review of Symptoms/Associated Signs and Symptoms: She describes no depressive symptoms. Symptoms of binging, purging and other indications of an eating disorder are convincingly denied. She denies obsessive, intrusive and persistent thoughts or compulsive, ritualistic acts. She denies thoughts of suicide or homicide.

Past Psychiatric History:

    Prior Psychiatric Disorder:
        She has a history of selective/traumatic mutism. Patient was diagnosed at age three. Patient has been in remission from diagnosis since age four.
        Outpatient Treatment: Penelope did receive outpatient mental health treatment for Selective

Mutism from age three to four.
Suicidal / Self Injurious: Penelope has no history of suicidal or self-injurious behavior. Current incident is first time of self-harm.
Addiction / Use History: Penelope denies any history of substance abuse.
Psychotropic Medication History: Psychotropic medications have never been prescribed for Penelope.

Past psychiatric history is otherwise entirely negative.

Social/Developmental History: Penelope is a student, age 13. She is American. She is a Jewish. Penelope has no siblings.

Employment History: Not applicable/Student.

Support System: Penelope has the social support of the following: Various family members including
Father, Grandmother, Grandfather (paternal grandparents)

Strengths/Assets: Penelope is not articulate and verbal, but willing to communicate via writing at this time.

Patient's Goals: "I just want to feel better."

Family History: Note: Information given by
                    patient's father.
                    Mother diagnosed with schizophrenia.
                    Aunt known to have anxiety. This

> family member is maternally related.
> Cousin carries diagnosis of anxiety. This
> family member is paternally related.

Family psychiatric history is otherwise negative. There is no other history of psychiatric disorders, psychiatric treatment or hospitalization, suicidal behaviors or substance abuse in closely related family members.

Medical History:
    Allergies: Citrus, dust, strawberries
    Current Medical Diagnoses: None
    Current Medications (non-psychotropic) include: None
    Past Medical History: As above

Medical history is otherwise negative, and Penelope has no other history of serious illness, injury, operation, or hospitalization. She does not have a history of asthma, seizure disorder, head injury, concussion or heart problems.

Diagnoses: The following Diagnoses are based on currently available information and may change as additional information becomes available.

Generalized Anxiety Disorder (Active)
Personal History of Self Harm, ICD 10

Instructions / Recommendations / Plan:
The risks and benefits of Psychotropic medications were explained to Penelope.

Cognitive Behavioral Therapy
Relaxation Techniques

Start Paxil 10 mg PO QAM (Anxiety)
Start Ambien CR 6.25 mg PO QHS (Insomnia)

Junea Grefla, MD

2.   DISCHARGE STATUS AND INSTRUCTIONS

Final Exam, Interval History, 12/21/2019

Penelope is stable. No psychiatric complaints are expressed. Symptoms of a Generalized Anxiety Disorder are not reported today.

The Zung Self-Rating Anxiety Scale quantifies a patient's level of anxiety. Penelope scored between 20-44 indicating that her anxiety level is in the normal range.

Final Exam, Mental Status Exam:

Penelope is calm, friendly, attentive, casually groomed, and relaxed. She still does not exhibit speech that is normal in rate, volume, and articulation. Flat affect and congruent with mood. Insight into illness is normal. Social judgment is intact. There are signs of recurrent anxiety whenever the subject of her mother is mentioned. There are no signs of hyperactivity or attention difficulties. Penelope has not exhibited self-harming behavior.

Discharge Diagnosis

Generalized Anxiety Disorder, 300.02 (Resolved)

Type of Discharge: Regular
Condition on Discharge: Greatly improved
Prognosis: Excellent
Medications at Discharge:
    Ambien CR 6.25 mg PO QHS
Medication Instructions: Patient should continue with current medications and follow up with primary care provider: Dr. Anderson.

Physical Activity: No limitations on physical activity

Dietary Instructions: Regular diet.

Other Instructions: The patient was advised to call treating physician and clinical psychologist if symptoms recur.

Emergency Contact: 212-292-1363

Junea Grefla, MD
Electronically Signed

Electronically Signed
By: John Meek, MD

WINTER

CHAPTER SEVENTEEN

"You can take her home," the therapist tells my father fifteen days later, after I'm examined and reexamined and have been given test after test after test. They think I'm asleep in my hospital bed, but I can hear them.

"Is she schizophrenic?" Dad asks, clearly terrified.

"She has a form of Selective Mutism. In her case, I believe it's Traumatic Mutism, triggered by a traumatic event."

"Are you sure?" Dad asks.

"I'm sure."

"It's just that her mother is schizophrenic."

IS schizophrenic. Is! Is! Somewhere I have a mother who is alive. My heart races. I'm so shocked that my eyes open but I quickly shut them. As long as they think I'm still asleep they'll keep on talking. I slit my eyes a bit so I can see them.

"Penelope was this way once before," Dad tells the doctor.

"I saw that on her chart. It was when your wife was first institutionalized. Correct?" Dad nods. "That's one of the reasons I believe this is Traumatic Mutism."

"What should I do with her when we get home?" Dad asks.

"Traumatic Mutism is a complex childhood anxiety

disorder," the doctor tells Dad. "There is no saying how long this will last. She could wake up with speech tomorrow once she's home in familiar surroundings. Has something happened recently? Besides the play, I mean. Is it related to her mother? She became agitated whenever I mentioned her mother."

"She hasn't seen my wife since she went into the asylum when Penelope was three. As far as Penelope knows, my wife is dead. I know my daughter had this before, but I never thought it would occur again, and I have no idea what to do." Dad is so flustered.

"The event with the play just doesn't seem traumatic enough to have triggered this episode," the doctor says. "Are you sure there is no other recent event?"

"Not that I'm aware of."

Of course, there *is* an event–a major event!–but Dad, as usual, is clueless, completely confident that he knows everything that ever happens to me. Meanwhile, he has been playing puppet master with my life–*and* my mother's!–and he thinks he can conceal this forever. I wish I could speak, so I could shout at him, tell him what a mess he's made of things, how it's all his fault. But instead, I just peep out from under my eyelids and watch while he flounders.

"What happens next?" he says.

"Start by home-schooling her and we'll arrange for a therapist to see her at least once a week. All her studies were within normal limits, including her EEG, head CT scan and the MRI of her brain. It's very important that you don't pressure her to speak. That will just increase her anxiety level. If there's no improvement in a month, we'll consider anti-anxiety medication."

Poor Dad! It's not like we have lots of extra money. I can hear his anxiety escalating. If I weren't so angry at my Dad, I might pity him. But, for now, the only person I feel sorry for is me!

CHAPTER EIGHTEEN

Christmas and Chanukah come and Dad is so desperate for me to speak. He buys me everything, even a new iPad, hoping I will just become myself again, but I am not sure who that someone is. Even television does nothing, and TV has always been my go-to, a place where Dad and I always found a show we could enjoy together. I love certain shows on Nextflix but the images float right above me, like with Zeina's Dad.

Every day, after school, Zeina stops by. "Talk to me," she begs.

I wish I could. I try to tell her with my eyes. I want to talk and I know I can talk, physically. But it's like something inside me has shut down. It's as though my thoughts are running on five lines at once and they're crashing into each other in some mental bottleneck that they used to be able to pass through. Describing it isn't easy. I'm not looking for attention and I'm not even being stubborn as I'm sure many people think.

Zeina won't give up. She fills me in on everything. What happened after the paramedics scooped me up and stuffed me into the ambulance during the awards ceremony. According to Zeina, Calvin tried to pick up and keep the play going after everything ground to a halt because the play's author was apparently dying in the aisle. He started feeding lines to Ava, but she began screaming, "How can you? How can you?" to Calvin. She had to be taken offstage by Reise, who was obviously terrified she would lose her job if all her pupils started dying because she stole my play without asking. That thought almost makes me smile. Almost, but not quite.

Johnny has been asking Zeina if she thinks he should come see me. He confided in Zeina that he is worried he had something to do with my breakdown because of that kiss. That kiss. That silly kiss. Sweet, goofy Johnny. He is so thoughtful, so sensitive. I wish I could tell him that kiss of his is the least of my worries these days.

It's so hard to see my grandparents during this time. When they come over for candle lighting for Chanukah, I don't even get out of bed. Zayde comes in, kisses my hands, and deposits all of his favorite Russian novelists on my bedspread. Among them is Isaac Babel, whose sweet melodies I loved, but didn't understand. Grandma brushes hair from my forehead. Her sad eyes show me how worried she is and so disappointed over the bat mitzvah that never was.

Zeina also comes over during Chanukah. I know she's desperate to hear from me, and even a little annoyed. "You're not the only one with a crazy parent, you know."

I open my mouth, thinking maybe something will come out of it, but nothing. She flashes a blank paper in front of me, inviting me to write a response, but what she doesn't get is there is nothing in me—an absence of anything, everything. She takes out her phone and flashes some crazy Instagram picture that looks Johnny, when he was younger, dressed as a clown.

Monday, 7 PM

Johnny: *Miss you in school; miss you in life*

Why is he IM'ing me? It is not like I'm going to answer.
I'm glad we're still friends, though.

Others start.

Dad: *How are you doin'?*

Does Dad *THINK* I am his friend? I don't answer.

Ava: *Miss you in school.*

Zeina: *Miss you more than anyone!*

I would like to smile from all these messages, would
like to laugh, too, but there is nothing inside me.

After Zeina leaves, Dad comes home. Randi, my
annoyingly chirpy tutor, reports to Dad.

"She wouldn't engage in *The Catcher in the Rye,* which
you never told me was her favorite book. I mean, I asked
if she understood Holden's feelings, and she stared me
down like there was nothing going on inside her head."

That's true enough. My mind is so blank these days.

"But we're going to give it another go tomorrow, aren't
we?" Randi gives me that encouraging smile with those
big, capped teeth that make me think of a cow's, and
prods, "Isn't that right, Penny?"

Talk about condescending! Of course, nobody has
bothered telling Randi to call me Pilar. Not that I care–

much.

*

That night I lie in the dark thinking about the word "crazy." I've noticed that I use it a lot, in a lot of different ways: "Randi is crazy if she thinks I'm gonna talk to her"; "That's crazy good"; "I'm crazy about him." And so on and so on. It means so many things that the word almost means nothing at all.

My mother was crazy. My mother *is* crazy. Now I, also, have slept overnight in a house for the mentally unstable. Like mother, like daughter? Am I headed down the same road as Star? Am I also crazy? Is that my fate—to grow up to spend the rest of my life in some mental facility?

The idea scares me so much that I tremble. I clasp my hands together and squeeze to force the shaking to stop. I won't let it happen. I won't! Maybe it's already happened. My classmates already thought I was kind of kooky. Now that they've all seen me banging my head against the floor in the performing arts center, they're sure I'm crazy. I'm really happy that I didn't post that selfie of me with that scarf wrapped around my head. It would just be more proof that I'm nuts.

Everyone needs to know that I'm a normal girl. Even if I'm not, I have to make certain everyone sees me as sane. No kooky scarves. Calling myself Pilar is my last name change. From now on I'm going to be the most in-the-box kid in school. If I pretend to be sane, then eventually, I will be sane. Maybe. And no more silence. I *want* to talk, but I can't. You know that circle on your computer that sometimes just spins and spins and spins when it can't

access the website you want? My mind feels like that. My
vocal cords can't access the words my mind wants to say.

CHAPTER NINETEEN

I am SO MAD at Dad these days. Since finding my mom's diary, I'm furious at him all the time.

IM'ing me:

Work is boring
Wuz up?
Work is boring
Do you want me to show you how circuits work?
Learn anything new today?
Do you want me to show you how circuits work?
So learn anything new today?
WUZ UP?

The last one pisses me off the most, when he tries to act like my friends and me, but—yet again—no words come out of me. Does he think he is cool or something? I *hate* that he thinks he is cool. First of all, unless he gets it—he does not—absolutely *no one* spells *WUZ UP* that way anymore. Do not try to be cool, Dad, especially when you are not a teenager. I try to type on my laptop, but my fingers slide off of the keys. He's being stupid but I don't have the words to tell him so.

It must be the end of the month, Zeina's birthday. I see

it on my Instagram feed. I see Instagram birthday messages written under a photo of Zeina smiling, standing in front of the school.

Zeina is a ballerina and a butterfly!!!
Happy birthday, butterfly!

That was from Johnny. Since when did Zeina become a butterfly?

Happy birthday Nina, ballerina
--Ava

Zeina, ballerina? Really? Sometimes Zeina is called Nina by weirdos at school who don't understand the name Zeina. These texts are not making me feel any better. I feel like my friends are going crazy. I hope nobody sends me anything this dumb when my birthday rolls around. What rhymes with Penny? Any. Many. Jenny. I think that's it. Figures–I don't even have a good name for birthday rhymes. Pilar, Superstar? Ugh–no. Sounds like crazy Andy Warhol.

I attempt to write my own birthday message to Zeina, but my heart isn't in it. The same logjam that's hit my voice is also in my fingers. Part of me wants to communicate with the outside world but a bigger part does not. Giving up, I shut my laptop. I feel like disappearing, just like my mother did. But she is alive and crazy and I think she really *LOVED* me.

I just used the word "crazy," like I often do. My friends are going "crazy." Do I think they're becoming mentally ill? Of course not! Then what do I mean? Are they acting in a strange way? Are they making no sense? Yes. Sort of. I'm going to pay more attention from now on to all the times I use the word "crazy" and make note of exactly what I actually mean by it.

CHAPTER TWENTY

Right now, Randi is into teaching me all about the Crusades of the Middle Ages. She says that a lot of our current international problems have roots going way, way back to when the British King sent knights to seize Jerusalem and also to forcibly convert the Muslims to Christianity. I seriously don't get why people would kill each other in the name of God. The Muslims killed in the name of Allah. The Catholic knights did all this looting and murdering in the name of God and all his holy saints.

I toy with the idea of being like a saint, whipping and starving myself–not to get closer to God, but to get closer to the pain my mother must have felt all these years, locked up in an institution. The thing is I begin to wonder if she *could* have left. Is my dad holding her as a prisoner there? Or—even worse—could she have left, but she chose not to?

Who knows? She's "crazy" (1), right? So, who knows why she does anything? That's the great thing about being "crazy" (1). You never have to explain why you do things you do. You're simply "crazy" (1).

(1) Crazy: Mentally ill

CHAPTER TWENTY-ONE

I am not answering anyone. I cannot read. I am sick of their texts, their messages. I cannot write. I cannot speak. I am mute; don't they get it?

Zeina: *Thinking about you all the time. Dad lost another job. Can you imagine? Cannot stand watching my mother's face while she watches my Dad—zombie-like—in front of the TV. I know you are reading this, Pilar. Can't you answer me?*

Ava: *What's the story? I heard you are starting to move around?*

Johnny: *No drama when you're not around, P.*

Zeina: *I'm gonna stop wearing this hijab if you don't cut this sh-t out!*

Calvin: *I miss your stories.*

Ava: *I miss your stories, too.*

Ellen: *I miss your stories three!*

Johnny: *School is so quiet without your voice.*

Zeina: *What can I do to get you to talk?*

Dad: *What can I do to get you to talk?*

Dad: *What can I do to get you to write?*
What can I do to get you to look into my eyes?
-Your loving Dad, forever and a day!

CHAPTER TWENTY-TWO

VISIT WITH THE THERAPIST

"Penny, look at me." I look at the therapist. I shrug my shoulders again.

"Tell me what you're feeling," she says. I shrug my shoulders.

"It might help if you could write it down," she says.

Does she want to watch me shrug my shoulders all day? I would tell her what I feel if I knew how to. I would talk if I knew how to, but right now I am an absence of speech. I am a pool of anger and sorrow. She can swim in it, if she wants.

"Here, write something," she presses on.

I have been saying nothing, writing nothing. But I do write something on the pad, hoping she will leave me alone. Why does she bother?

"O," I write.

I suppose this is sufficient, since she leaves. It wasn't a word, nor a letter. It was a drawing of the great big hole that's inside of me.

CHAPTER TWENTY-THREE

At my window, the snow swirls angrily. It rages, blasting gusts of icy white onto the glass.

"Next week will be the end of February and it will be two months of this shit," Zeina shouts at me. "And I'm not talking about the weather. I am talking about your shit."

She and Johnny came over together after school and are now standing at the end of my bed. I do not feel supported because they're here. I feel ganged up on.

"And—by the way—you're not the only one who has sucky things going on in your life. I mean, really!" Zeina adds.

I open my mouth, feeling the words bubbling beneath the surface, but when I try to unearth what I want to say, I can't. Randi, my tutor, told me in one of her motivational pep talks—the ones that make me wish I could run, screaming, from the room, if only I could scream—that if we could put everybody's problems in a big pile on the middle of the floor and take a good look at them, chances are I'd want my own problems back. But at the moment it's hard to believe that's really true—even though I know Zeina's problems and I know Johnny's problems, and they are real and painful problems, too. All the same—I'd swap for just about anyone else's life right now.

"I'm going to stop wearing this shitty hijab until you

start talking to me!" she says.

She knows I hate her to break with tradition. I like things I can depend on. Although what I also like about Zeina is she is such a non-conformist, and so proud to be one, too.

Johnny stands next to Zeina. "And I might start putting garlic in my famous chocolate chip pancakes if you don't stop all this not-talking stuff."

I think that would be "crazy" (2) but I am mute. Besides, I know he's not gonna do it. I shake my head no, but it is a feeble attempt at reaching out. Still, it's something, and Zeina starts jumping up and down on the bed with Johnny, chanting "Talk-to-me! Talk-to-me!"

They are "crazy" (2). I have such mad, crazy friends.

That night I have trouble sleeping. Mostly, I dream about my mother, wondering if she had been allowed to be who she wanted to be—maybe an imaginary king—if that would have made a difference. In my dream, I am sitting in her kingly lap, and I feel her strong, warm arms embrace me.

"I love you!" she tells me.

"Then why did you leave?"

"I had no choice."

"I love you, too," I tell her, even though I have no idea who this mother is, since she is dressed in a royal robe.

In the next two weeks, things—little things—gradually start improving. I can't write, I can't speak, but I start responding to Randi's lessons. I had been taking psychology as an elective, and Randi, in her enthusiasm, decides to use my textbooks to renew my interest. Now,

(2) Crazy: wacky, unconventional, in a good way.

though, knowing what I've learned about my mother's mental illness, the subject creeps me out, in a way it never had before.

"The mind," Randi says, "can be weirdly adaptive. Let's say you want to blackout something—you are able to do that and disconnect from the world. That's how people protect themselves; it's a kind of self-preservation."

I know what she's getting at, what she's trying to do. I heard my dad talking to her the other night, how he could not figure out for the life of him why I just stopped speaking.

"And writing," he had exclaimed. "My daughter's a writer. I mean me—I'm scientific; everything is logical, but she lives in another zone, another space. She even changed her name to Pilar, since it has a more romantic ring to it."

I was so impressed that he was impressed with what I do. Like it was a WOW moment, a double "crazy" (3) moment.

"Why such silence? I know she is super mad at me for letting her teacher perform her play, but I told her I was sorry dozens of times. And the therapists? Randi, so help me, I know therapy is not quite a science, but they have no idea what is going on with her. True, they've come up with a diagnosis, but that is about it. It's getting me annoyed."

Stupid Dad! I want to ask him about the diary. What about your wife? What about my mother?

I snuck into the living room at the time I heard them speaking, since I didn't like the hushed whispers they were using. And guess what? I was blown off the top. If there

(3) Crazy: The best

was any time for me to scream, this was it, but when I opened my mouth, nothing came out!

There they were, my Dad and Randi—oh, my God, she is almost his age, but I hadn't realized it until that moment. And there they were, on the couch, faces so close together they were almost touching, a bottle of wine between them. In another moment, it would turn into a kiss.

Could things get any "crazier"? (4).

(4) Crazier: Wild, out of control

CHAPTER TWENTY-FOUR

The March rain pounds on my window and I roll over in bed because my phone dings with a text. Dad again, with his silly jokes. He tells me that he just became friends with Donald Trump on Facebook. He uses 'LOL'! I told him once before I hate when he pretends to be cool. I tell him this is *not* funny. Why is he cracking all these stupid jokes? Why is he using expressions like LOL?! It is so on my nerves.

Another, ding. Another text from Dad.

Please, please, please talk to me. Just one word would suffice!

I feel like *The Little Engine That Could*, one of my favorite children's books from when I was younger. *I wish I could. I wish I could. I wish I could.* Sure, I would like to say, *I think I can. I think I can. I think I can*, but I can't.

Later that day I can't pay attention to Randi's lessons. I'm ticked off at her because she's making a play for my dad. Or maybe it's the other way around. Whatever–she should know it's unacceptable! Her eyes narrow questioningly as she studies me. She knows something is wrong because I barely look at her. Can she guess what it is?

The next day, Saturday, Johnny comes into my room with a surprise-breakfast in bed. He's holding a tray with chocolate chip pancakes with homemade whipped cream and fruit on top. I know it is all homemade since he loves to cook. He has a lot in common with my dad. He must have talked my Dad into letting him sneak into our kitchen while I was asleep. Dad must be really desperate if he let somebody else use his sacred stove! Maybe Johnny has a lot in common with my mom, too. But he loves to sing, which is more like Dad. I think. I don't know.

"Uptown funk don't give to ya! Funk!" Johnny isn't even singing the correct lyrics.

He pulls up in front of the bed and presents the pile of steaming pancakes with a flourish and a comical bow designed to yank a laugh out of me.

"Dontcha want to know if I put in the garlic?" he asks.

I'm supposed to smile at his joke, but it doesn't work; nothing does, except when Grandma and Zayde visit.

Grandma is no help at all, screaming and crying, "Vey es mir" over and over like a chant, a mantra. Dad just drags her out of the room, but Zayde stays behind and opens up his Bible, his beloved Bible. He starts to read, from "Song of Songs."

"I picked this because it's like a fairy tale between a prince and princess," he tells me. "Close your mind and picture them talking to each other. Give that busy mind a rest and just enjoy."

SHE:
Let him kiss me with the kisses of his mouth-
For your love is more delightful than wine.
Pleasing is the fragrance of your perfumes;

Your name is like perfume poured out.
No wonder the young women love you!
Take me away with you—let us hurry!
Let the king bring me into his chambers.

FRIENDS:
We rejoice and delight in you;
We will praise your love more than wine.

SHE:
While the king was at his table,
My perfume spread its fragrance.
My beloved is to me a sachet of myrrh
Resting between my breasts.
My beloved to me is a cluster of henna blossoms
From the vineyards of En Gedi.

HE:
How beautiful you are, my darling!
Oh, how beautiful!
Your eyes are doves.

SHE:
How handsome you are, my beloved!
Oh, how charming!
And our bed is verdant.

HE:
The beams of our house are cedars;
Our rafters are firs.

Listening to Zayde's voice somehow calms me, and it

is like I am resting in some spectacular dream. I cuddle into his arms and feel, for one short moment, an inner peace I have not felt for a long, long time.

"Thank you," I whisper, dozing off to sleep.

CHAPTER TWENTY-FIVE

In the morning I awaken with the idea that I've spoken. Was it a dream? And then it comes back to me. Yes! Yes! Yes! I spoke. Did Zayde hear me? Does he know? I bet not. His hearing isn't good. I haven't heard my own voice in so long. I hadn't even intended to speak. The words just slid out of my lips, straight from my heart. I'm not sure I can do it again.

"Hello?" I whisper, my voice cracks, brittle, but mine. Why did it happen? Maybe it's just time.

Outside my window there are buds on the dogwood tree. How do they know it's almost spring? It's time, I guess. I have no idea, really. My heart explodes with joy. I can speak. I say small words—*it, can, but*—just to test myself, to be sure it wasn't a mistake, an oddity, a once-only thing. No! It's real!

I can't wait to speak for Dad. In my excitement, I forget to be mad at him. Suddenly, the Cowardly Lion—Dad—dances into my room. Dad likes to sing, not dance, but here he is, dancing, too!

"I'm afraid there's no denyin', I'm just a dandylion, a fate I don't deserve." He dances around a little and then belts out, "I'd be brave as a blizzard / I'd be gentle as a lizard / I'd be clever as a gizzard / if the wizard is a wizard who will serve."

And, like magic, I'm laughing—real laughter, with a sound. It starts out small and quiet but explodes till I am laughing and crying and also uttering, over and over, "You are crazy" (8). The words are so fluid, as if they had been there all along, just ready to burst out. It makes me wonder if things are ever truly lost—or if they are just buried temporarily, almost put in storage, prepared to be sent into the world when they are ready.

Dad stares at me, his mouth open, tears brimming in his eyes.

"Say it again," he pleads in a voice so low I can barely hear him.

I start crying, too. I don't want to be mad at him now. Only happy. Anger can wait until later.

(8) Crazy: Madcap; zany

CHAPTER TWENTY-SIX

It turns out that later is lunchtime. Maybe being hungry brings out the crabby, angry parts of me. I'm not sure, as we sit on the couch watching some men and women arguing over politics. Dad clicks off the TV.

"I know all this political talk can really get you down. There are so many awful problems in the world."

"That's not it," I say.

"Well, something's bothering you," he replies. "That's a pretty fierce scowl on your face. What's going on?"

"It's you," I tell him. "You're what's going on. You're what's up!"

His temples flush. "Me? Do you want to talk about the play?"

"We'll get to the play," I say. "But we have way more stuff to discuss before that."

"Cut me a little slack, would you?" Dad says. "Perhaps you don't realize how terrified I've been."

"Not so terrified that you couldn't make out with Randi."

Silence. I didn't plan to bring that up right away since I really want to talk about something more important. "Why did you lie to me?"

"How did I lie? This thing with Randi-it's very new, and I don't know where it's going yet, and-listen. I'm entitled not to discuss every detail of my personal life with my daughter. And I admit, I was wrong about the play. I thought it would make you happy but obviously I was very wrong. I said I was sorry at least a hundred times. If I were Oz, I would flip the curtain back and do right by you."

"The wizard was a liar, too."

Dad has no idea what I'm really talking about. He doesn't know I found the diary. My phone is going off with messages like mad, but I turn it off. Dad and I need to have this conversation. I want to have it like "crazy" (9). Right now!

"I found my mother's diary."

"You what?" His mouth is open so wide that I can see deep into the empty tunnel at the back of this throat. "I kept it so well hidden."

"But I found it!"

"By going through my drawers. I don't like that." He tries to shift the blame to me, but I am onto that trick, since I use it myself.

I put it right back where it belongs–on him. "Not as sucky as telling me my mother's dead!"

"You're right, yes." He casts his gaze down toward the ground. "I was saving it until you got older. I thought you would understand things better."

"But you lied to me!"

"I did it to protect you!"

"What, Dad! Why? How? I feel way worse now, so what protection?"

"Shoot me." His standard 'I said I was wrong, now stop talking about it' response.

(9) Crazy: Mad, urgent

I make a POW sign. Of course I wouldn't, even if I had a gun. But I feel the urge to just hit him and hit him and hit him.

"Did you think I'd go 'crazy' (10) if I knew?"

"I guess not."

"But she was 'crazy' (11), right?"

"If that's the word you want to use. I would prefer to call her schizophrenic. Do you know what that means?"

Wow, I had been using that word so much in my blog. About the world. About the weather. But never about my mother.

"Are you sure she wasn't just sad? Maybe confused because she couldn't be what she wanted to be—a man? I don't mean to be harsh here, Dad, but like, what if I told Johnny, 'I'm not gonna let you be yourself, because it doesn't suit *my* idea of you for you to be yourself'? He would probably get pretty bent out of shape."

"It's not entirely the same situation with your mother as it is with Johnny. Johnny knew what was bothering him. Your Mom—no one knew if her confused desires made her 'flip.' Sometimes she called herself Star, her female name. Other times she was Stavan, her male name. Other times she was Mr. Lasky. She would just slip into one of those personas or the other, without realizing it. She was not like Johnny. He knows who he is."

Depression is creeping back. Dad doesn't want to hear me at all. I start to think maybe we do become unbalanced or lose words when people don't get them, don't listen to them, the way everyone pushed and nagged at me to write

(10) Crazy: Bonkers
(11) Crazy: Mentally ill

my play, even though I wasn't ready. It's easy to lose your voice when you are silenced.

"I don't know. I'm not a psychiatrist. The doctors call her a paranoid schizophrenic. She hears voices in her head that tell her to do strange things. She becomes violent. She's a danger to herself and to others," Dad says.

I think about Johnny. Would he go "crazy" (12) if he was forced to live life as a girl and not change? What if somebody told me, "You can't be a writer"? Yes—that might definitely send me over the edge.

"Was my mom always like that?" I ask.

"Schizophrenia usually shows up during one's late teens. Your Mom had no friends at that point."

"Wow," I say softly. "But you married her."

"I did not see what was right in front of my eyes. How can I make it up to you?" There goes Dad. Put a Band-Aid on it, and pretty soon we'll pretend there was never a boo-boo.

"You can't."

He looks petrified. I relent. "Oh, Daddy. Just tell me where she is and take me there."

"Now?"

"No, soon. When I'm ready."

He doesn't get it. I am scared. What if I am mentally ill, too? I never knew my mother—only vague memories. And then I read this diary from a woman who was clearly struggling with her identity. What about my identity? I am terrified.

"I can do that. It is easy enough, I guess," he says. "By the way, I want you to go back to school on Monday."

(12) Crazy: Have a mental breakdown, lose touch with reality

Really—having to face everyone? Having to explain?
"No," I say. "I can't. I'm not ready. It's too soon."

*

The next day at breakfast, I share what has been brooding in me for months.

"What came first—the chicken or the egg?"

"About what?" Dad asks. "We haven't played this game in a very long time."

"Well, now I'm ready, which does not mean I have forgiven you!" He curls into himself like a turtle. "What came first—me, or my mother's mental illness?"

He *umphs*. And moves around like a Mexican jumping bean. "What are you asking?"

"Did the pregnancy make her go bonkers?"

Silence. More silence. "Come on, Dad; spit it out!"

"She was way off before she got pregnant. I just didn't want to see it. I wanted a child so much."

"Okay, so the pregnancy made her worse?"

"Maybe."

"What does that mean, Dad?"

"Giving birth triggered her first really severe episode of losing touch with reality. There were more episodes after that, and the voices kept getting louder in her head."

"What does that mean? She was schizophrenic— wasn't she?"

"Yes, but it's complicated."

"Isn't everything?" I ask.

"More so with this."

"So, what came first, Daddy?"

No answer. And I leave it at that, since that might be

the truth. Dad clears the dishes from the table.

"I'm waiting for a return call from Dr. Shoane. I'm hoping she can fit us in for a special visit tomorrow."

I nod, at a loss for words. My throat grows dry and I'm suddenly very tired. I want to go back to bed. Talking to Dr. Shoane will require so many words that I just don't have yet. What's the use?

Joan Shoane, PhD
Client initials: PL
Date of initial session: 12/06/2019
Date of most recent session: 3/20/2020
Total number of client sessions: Therapist has been seeing the client since December 2019, 1-2x a week
Date intake report written 12/12/2019

I.   Identifying information & current life setting

Client has been attending sessions with therapist since December 2019. She has an active diagnosis of Select/Traumatic Mutism, with no history of substance abuse. Client has no long-term history of self-harm, but self-harmed by head-banging in December. She currently resides in a private home with her father. Client has been residing here from birth till present day.

Client comes into sessions neatly dressed and well-groomed–usually wearing jeans, a colorful sweater, and boots. Client has a friendly demeanor, but is guarded.

Although client is scheduled to attend sessions every Tuesday and Friday from 8:30 am to 9:30 am, she was reluctant to come at first, often arriving late, or missing the session entirely, but has begun to come on time, and is missing fewer scheduled sessions recently. She will be changing them to a later time as she is returning to school.

Client's living situation has been a growing stressor in her life and has been the focus of many of our recent sessions. Client has begun communicating with therapist verbally at times, but will revert to writing her thoughts at other times. Client reports that she is not comfortable talking to her father about what she is thinking and feeling. Client claims she is unable to sleep well due to inability to speak with her father.

Her two primary concerns are 1) Mending the relationship with her father and 2) Her approaching return to school. The issues regard her inability to express her true feelings to her father and her terror at the idea of returning to school.

Client admits to having felt overwhelmed with stress and anxiety upon seeing her play performed, but states, "It is more than that" when questioned. Client is not comfortable discussing her mother and will often put her head down and stay silent until the topic has been changed.

In the past, when the client was experiencing problems at her residence or school, she would verbalize her concerns or journal about them. Client states that she has never expressed irritability as she does now. In addition, it appears that in the past she used to utilize her family relationships as a support system and as a means of coping with the problems in her daily life. Client stated she would speak to her father and paternal grandparents on a consistent basis. However, more recently, she is expressing conflicting relationships with her friends (with whom she is unable to feel a former closeness). The client does not seem to be using her family relationships as a resource for coping at this time. Client's hostile attitude towards discussing her mother has created a conflict between her father and during therapy, and this conflict has yet to be resolved. Most recent sessions have centered on the interpersonal conflicts between her and her father.

The client's psychological conflicts appear, in great part, due to the loss of her mother. In conceptualizing the client from standard stages of grief models, she appears in the second stage of grief, which is the "anger" stage. Often at this stage, a person mourning can display anger towards oneself or towards other people, especially those who are close to them (i.e., Father).

In addition, client's attitude of learned helplessness and inaction in the residence could stem from the fact that she was unable to "control" her mother's absence. The "control" here is not in the sense that she couldn't prevent her mother's disappearance, but more in the sense that she was completely uninvolved and powerless in the decision-making process as a young child. This sense of powerlessness she experienced during her mother's disappearance may have caused her to stop speaking then, and fostered a passive mindset and the faulty perception that she has no control over certain outcomes or situations. When she saw her play being performed after she refused permission to have it produced, she again felt that belief of no control. This kind of mentality would explain why she remains stagnant and is still not speaking at home or in school, but is progressing quickly in speaking in all other environments.

II.   Counseling/Treatment Plan

The main goals for our individual sessions are 1) Discuss

coping skills that the client can use when dealing with interpersonal conflicts at home or school.

The client will need to develop a set of coping skills for various situations at her home including: Ways to be verbally assertive. Assertiveness skills, such as "I" statements, would allow her to clearly express her thoughts towards her father or others. By being more proactive at home, she can start to regain her sense of control and understand she is not the victim in her situations.

2) In addition, client will need to continue to attempt to share her issues regarding her mother, so she can receive feedback and support. Currently, she is working on writing down what she feels when hearing certain statements about her mother in sessions, such as, "I wish I could speak to my mom now," and "My dad won't talk to me about my mom."

SPRING

CHAPTER TWENTY-SEVEN

IM: Let everyone know I am returning to school Monday.

Two seconds later, the phone starts buzzing like "crazy" (13). I answer it.

"Oh, my God; oh, my God; oh, my God!" Zeina shouts into the phone.

"You are hurting my ears. Just because I couldn't talk doesn't mean there was ever anything wrong with my hearing, remember?"

"Of course I remember. I've been there nearly every day. Did you realize that?"

"Of course, I know. And I'm really grateful."

"It's 'crazy' (14) how this happened to you. What was going on in your head?"

I don't know—not exactly. I'm trying to figure out how to describe what happened to me, when I really don't know what happened to me. I sigh.

Zeina hesitates. "It's just—you know. You scared me so bad. It was almost like—well. My Dad and everything. I was afraid I was gonna lose you, too. What happened? What made you shut down like that?"

(13) Crazy: wildly
(14) Crazy: unexpected; unforeseen

I feel awful. Of course it must have been horrible for Zeina.

"I don't even know. There was a lot inside, believe me, but when I tried to talk, to write, nothing came out."

"That is so weird!" Zeina digests this. When she speaks again, she sounds so hopeful. "Do you think–do you think maybe my Dad might get better all of a sudden, like you did?"

I can't think of what to say to that. I mean, how should I know? I'm not a psychiatrist! And even Full-of-Baloney Dr. Joanie admits she has no real clue what turned off the language in me, and what turned it back on again. But how can I hurt Zeina by saying that? Luckily, my phone vibrates. Why is Randi calling me? I am so done with this relationship. Still, it's a way out of this conversation with Zeina.

"Oh, Zeina. I gotta take this. It is my tutor. Later!"

"Oh, sure! Later!"

"I just heard from your Dad. I am so happy for you!" That chirpy voice.

"Thanks!" Thud.

Silence. What Randi doesn't know is how easy silence is for me now. As much as I *love* language, I have learned to live without it. I learned how you can love something, then discard it. Like my mom did to me? No–they made her leave, she didn't want to. It isn't the same.

"Your dad says you're not going back to school right away?" She tries again.

"No."

"I'll see you later, then." And again.

"Yeah. See you." Click.

Dad sticks his head in my room. "How's pancakes for

breakfast, Dorothy?"

"Terrific, Scarecrow."

Even though I'm acting friendly, I'm still so angry, so hurt, so confused that I just can't wrap my brain around how this will all end up. Plus, I am just getting used to hearing my voice. It is just too weird!

I eat breakfast and finish just as the front doorbell rings. There is Johnny outside my door. "Missed you!"

He is so handsome. It's like in the past three months, I didn't speak or write, and I also didn't see. When I wasn't paying attention, Johnny got busy developing a new "crazy" (15) look. I like it: hair dyed jet-black, tight snakeskin print jeans, Drake t-shirt. Black Chucks. But even in this get-up, I don't feel the chemistry. He is my very good buddy. That's it.

"Just stopped by for a hug!"

It is one secret of our friendship that I will never tell–that he's grinning at me, but his eyes are a little wet. It is one secret of our friendship that I will never tell–that deep, deep down, Johnny is a total mush.

"That I can do!" I give him a giant hug. "Getting a little burned out on speaking."

"No worries. This is all I wanted. I let everyone know you will be back in school on Monday. That okay?"

"Great!" And it is, actually. Now I can't back out. "Wanna stay for pancakes?"

"Can't. Meeting someone for coffee."

"A *date*? With *whom*?"

"You'll have to ask me at school!" He smirks and races out the door as I throw a pillow at him.

(15) Crazy: Wild

Left alone, I am scared to go back to school—and a little embarrassed, too. And part of me feels funny Johnny is going on a date, even a little possessive.

A few more calls from all my wonderful friends. It's comforting to know that they'll be there for me on my first day back. And yet, how do I begin to tell them about my mother?

The Lost Language Of Crazy

Announcement: my blog will no longer be called Over the Rainbow. When I called it that, it seemed to me that all the wisdom of the world was contained in *The Wizard of Oz*. Things have happened to me since then, though. Things have gotten "crazy" (16) and now I am more interested in learning what "crazy" (17) really means. We say it all the time. I do. What, though, do we really mean by it?

The country is schizophrenic. The weather's schizophrenic. I wrote about this a while ago, before I ever knew my mother is schizophrenic. I haven't met her yet, but her diary said she hears voices, and they make her do wild, unpredictable "crazy" (18) things. My father has been filling in some of the blanks. He said one time she was shopping at Macy's; I wasn't even a year old. She went into the men's department and was ready to steal a tuxedo; she insisted it belonged to her in another lifetime. Sometimes she is a king and sometimes she is a queen; a prince and a princess; a man and a woman. My dad says those voices told her to do frightening things when I was little, so he was really scared after a while to leave me alone with her. It seems like maybe if he let her be a man, she would have been just fine, but Daddy says that's making it way too simple. So maybe not.

When I Googled schizophrenia, it said it is a REAL condition caused by the wiring in the brain. My friend insists her dad's wiring is off, that he's schizophrenic, too, but I don't think so. He is just sad. Sad and mad. Depression, though, when it's severe and uncontrollable, is another mental illness. At least that's what I have read.

When they went through my files, they discovered I had an episode of mutism when I was little, right after my mom left. Does that make me schizophrenic?
This might be the last time I write for a very long time. It is getting me too upset.

And Johnny is NOT like my mom, my Dad reminds me. Johnny has never been confused about who he is. My mom was. And schizophrenia maybe had nothing to do with this confusion.

Or maybe it did.

(16) Crazy: Wild
(17) Crazy: A word used to describe many different conditions
(18) Crazy: Hard to understand

CHAPTER TWENTY-EIGHT

I'm back at school and everyone is making such a fuss that it is driving me "crazy" (19). Ava is hugging and kissing me; Johnny is hugging and kissing me; even Ms. Reise is hugging and kissing me.

Zeina comes in and I can't believe it. She has her hijab off. Her thick dark hair flows to her shoulders. She looks so different! We stare at each other. Zeina doesn't hug me, which isn't surprising. That is never her way-not in public. I know how happy she is to have me back, though I really don't feel so back. She smiles, though, and I smile in return.

During first period English, Reise hands out papers and asks us to write about journeys. I suppose you can say I have been on a long one—sad and far away, yet I can't write about it. I stare at the blank piece of paper for a really long time. Zeina pinches my arm from her seat behind me.

"Are you okay?"

"Not really? And you?"

"Not really, but we have to do this, Pilar."

"Yeah, I'll get to it."

But I don't get to it. I feel emptied, like all I once had inside of me is gone. I am that blank sheet of paper. Maybe

(19) Crazy: Ridiculous

it's going to take a long, long time to fill it. Johnny shrugs his shoulders at me, like "what's up?" There is a giant smile pasted on his face. He is "crazy" (20). It's good to know he is thrilled to see me, but everyone has to get that I'm not so thrilled to see myself.

"I'm sorry," I whisper to Ms. Reise when she sees nothing on my paper. Oddly enough she is so okay, too okay.

I want to shout at her to treat me like everyone else. Stop it!

"No worries. Just take your time!"

I'm now that weird kid that I totally do not want to be. I want to be Pilar Normal—the most average girl in Middle School 55.

"Let's go for pizza," Calvin suggests after school.

Last time I saw them together, Calvin and Ava couldn't get their hands off of each other, but now she is barely acknowledging his existence. And I am speechless. Them no longer being a thing feels too "crazy" (21) to me, but everything is. Whatever–I'm in no mood to listen to Calvin unloading his relationship woes. Zeina has taken off her hijab. Johnny is–maybe–seeing somebody, but he won't tell me who it is. And me? I'm changed, too. The difference is, I feel like I'm the only one who's changed for the worse.

(20) Crazy: Ridiculous
(21) Crazy: Totally unexpected

CHAPTER TWENTY-NINE

It takes me a whole week to muster up the courage to visit my mom, who apparently lives in a Psychiatric Facility in Coney Island. Zeina offers to come with me, but I want to do this on my own. Dad wants to come in with me.

"Have you visited her since she went in there?" I ask. "C'mon, Dad," I prod when he doesn't answer.

"You know we're divorced."

"I figured, but what does that have to do with visiting her?"

"I suppose nothing." He looks awkward and ashamed. "In the beginning I visited her every week, and then...."

Silence. "And then I stopped," he says.

"Why?"

"It was uncomfortable."

I don't really understand, but still I say, "I'm sorry, Dad." We hug each other. He starts to cry.

When he finally stops, he asks me, "How is your writing going?"

"It's not."

"What do you mean?"

"When I got my voice back, I wrote a piece, but it creeped me out to write. So I plan on staying away. "

"Maybe you will soon."

"Maybe. Who knows?"

And maybe I'll fly to the moon. And maybe global warming is a hoax, even though it is April and today is eighty-five degrees. And maybe I will finish my play, though the possibility seems more and more unlikely.

We ride in the car in silence. I look out the window. We have been here so many times. Coney Island is one of my happiest places in the world. The seagulls. The white foam on the waves. The salt tang on my lips when I breathe in the sea air, and the smell of hot dogs and candy apples.

"Can we stop at the beach first?" I ask.

"Sure."

I want to dip my feet in the water. I want to feel my toes in the sand. And when we get there, my dad stands off in the distance, on the boardwalk, smiling at me doing my thing, but still feeling so sad.

"Come on in, Dad," I call to him.

He shouts back, "You're the one who loves the water. Not me."

Yes, I love it. Can't wait to go in. And, for the first time in a long time, I feel hopeful. Soon I will bring my friends here with me. We'll go to Luna Park and ride the Ferris wheel. Perhaps I will bring Zeina with me to visit my mom. She has already offered. Coney Island is funky, filled with every race, age, gender you can imagine. Johnny once shared with me how at home he feels at Coney Island because sometimes you can't even tell, at the Mermaid Parade, who's a guy, who's a girl, and who is in between. There are so many people like that!

"Okay, Dad, ready to go." I dry off my toes on an old t-shirt.

"Are you sure you don't want me to go with you?" he asks, as I drag my sandy, wet body beside him into the car, something he would ordinarily get annoyed with, but now seems cool about. I nod. I'm sure.

"I'll wait for you downstairs," he says.

"No worries, Dad. Sure, wait for me. Actually, no—leave. I want to do this on my own. I want to take the subway home. I do have to ask you another favor, though."

"What?"

"I need you to set another date for my bat mitzvah. I need for you to call the rabbi, even though I should probably do it, but I'm embarrassed."

He looks eager, hopeful, expectant. "Sure, when?"

"Not till the fall."

"You'll be in high school then."

"So what? I am just not ready to tackle the chants, the prayers, any of it right now. I'm just trying to figure things out. And make it *late* fall." He looks like a wounded puppy. "Daddy, I am doing this for you, Grandma, and Zayde, not for me."

Again, that wounded puppy look. "Do you not want to do it at all?" he asks.

"No. I want to. I'm doing it for you guys!"

The car turns off the highway and into a parking lot. It feels too soon. It feels like I've been waiting all my life. Am I ready? Doesn't matter–we're here, and I'm doing this!

"Wow, Pilar. You are really growing up!" Dad looks happy and sad, both at the same time.

"Sort of. When I try."

I get out of the car, blow a kiss and get ready. Deep breaths. I enter the automatic glass doors. The psychiatric hospital is not as scary as I thought it would be. I don't know what I expected–something out of a movie, maybe. But it's just a regular-looking building, a little shabby, a little worn, like all the other old buildings next to the ocean. The lobby has fluorescent lights, which is kind of awful. Everything looks horrible under fluorescent lighting. I step up to the reception desk, trying not to show how nervous I am, and ask which room my mother is in. There's a brief hassle about IDs and being an unaccompanied minor, but finally the woman with the drugstore reading glasses sliding down her nose takes pity, hands me a visitor sticker, and points me toward the elevators.

I take the longest elevator ride of my life. It doesn't just seem that way—it is! That's because when I get to the sixth floor, I hit the lobby button. At the lobby, I hit the button for the sixth floor once more. And at six, I go down to the lobby again. I do this two more times. I might have done it all day except I figured people might start to notice and the last thing I need to do is to be called out by some official for being "crazy" (22), especially when I am already in a mental facility. So, I step out on the sixth floor. Left? Right? Which way do I go? It would be awful to wind up in the wrong room! I almost wish I'd let Dad come along. But then I see the arrows with the room numbers above them painted on the wall.

The walls are chipped and dirty. People are screaming; I never knew there could be so many volumes of a scream. I take a deep breath and head for Room 604. The place smells like bleach. It occurs to me that there might be a "Sheets" poem I could write about this. Immediately I

(22) Crazy: Deranged

stomp on the idea. Thinking like that doesn't help my new normal identity.

I move quietly down the hall, feeling like a ghost. Most of the doors are closed but some of them are open. Most of the people I see are asleep in a chair. Some gaze out a window. Others watch TVs that are mounted near the ceilings. They look "crazy" (23) to me, but maybe because I am scared.

My mother's door is open and I enter another sparsely furnished room with a high TV. There is this thin woman, dressed in overalls with a t-shirt underneath, sitting by the window looking out onto Ocean Parkway, where trees are loose-limbed and huge.

"Hi," I say to her.

She gazes at me with no sign of recognition. I know those eyes; they are large and green—my eyes—but they have lost their spark. She wears no makeup. Her hair is gray with streaks of reddish-brown. It is back in an elastic. I wonder if she is Star or Stavan right now.

"It's me—Penelope."

She's still blank. "Penelope who?"

I swallow hard. What should I say? Your long-lost daughter? Maybe I shouldn't have come. This suddenly feels like a mistake. A really "crazy" (23) person in the hallway starts to shout curse words. My mother is quiet, placid, not the "firecracker" my dad described.

"I'm Penelope Lasky. I have the same last name as you."

"My Penny?" She gets up and her eyes flash.

"Your Penny."

(23) Crazy: Insane

She hugs me so tightly that I can't breathe.

"You know, when I was looking out the window, I was looking for you!"

I laugh.

"Seriously!"

And then she says something remarkable. "I love you so much," she says, still hugging me really tight.

I don't respond. I'm shocked. Amazed. Am I dreaming? She stares at me, smiling. At first. Her eyebrows slowly furrow and a cloud comes across her eyes.

"I've been waiting because I have a secret to tell you," she says, dropping her voice to a whisper.

"What is it?" I ask. I bend my head toward her. My heart races. What will she reveal to me?

"God is dead," she says. She peers into my eyes. "What do you think of that?"

"I... uh... I don't. No. I don't think..."

"GOD IS DEAD!" she screams. She grabs the pillow from her bed and tears at the seams, biting it. Then she slaps the window with the pillow, hitting it over and over. "GOD IS DEAD!"

I step back, confused and terrified.

A nurse in green scrubs appears and I'm so happy to see her. She puts her arm around my mother.

"Settle down, Star. Put down the pillow."

With one hand still on my mother, the nurse stretches to her limit and presses a button above the bed.

Very quickly a male nurse in white scrubs appears holding a two small paper cups. He hands one cup to the other nurse.

"Take this, Star," the woman nurse says.

My mother shakes her head violently. "GOD IS DEAD!

PENELOPE LASKY IS DEAD! I AM DEAD!"

Both nurses hold onto her and gently, firmly guide Star into her chair.

"HELP! I'M DROWNING!" my mother screams. "LIFEGUARD! I NEED THE LIFEGUARD."

"Here comes the lifeguard," the female nurse tells her.

Another male nurse appears with a needle pointed at the ceiling. He injects the needle's contents into my mother's arm muscle near her shoulder. My mother slumps in the chair. She's calm and her expression goes blank. The male nurse looks toward the door.

"Maybe you had better leave for now," he suggests.

I'm relieved that he has asked me to leave. "Bye, Mom," I say softly, backing to the door.

I don't know if she hears me as she gazes at the ceiling. Next thing I know I am speed-walking down the hall toward the elevator, away, away, away from this madness.

CHAPTER THIRTY

"How was it?" my Dad asks later that day.

"I can't really talk about it. It feels too hard to describe." Take a hint, Dad.

Of course, he can't. Dad is much too eager. "Tell me. Try."

"In the beginning she seemed glad to see me. She was pretty normal." Then I tell him how she flipped out and had to be sedated at the end.

Dad nods, looking sad and serious. "So, you see how it is with her? Was she Star or Stavan?"

I nod at him and my eyes brim with tears. I tilt my head up at the ceiling so that my tears won't spillover. It's the last thing I want. Then I recall my mother's blank face studying the ceiling and I look down. I quickly wipe my eyes with my hand.

"Star, I guess. No one called her Stavan." A tear ran down my cheek and I whisked it away.

"I'm sorry, honey," Dad says.

"You warned me," I reply.

Once we're home, I force a smile, and leave dad in the kitchen to go to my computer in my bedroom. All these group chats pop up on my screen. Zeina calls, begging me to let her come with me next time I visit my mother. Ha. This from the girl who stonewalled me from meeting her dad. I say that I'll think about it and take the break-through call from Johnny.

"Let me go with you next time, please, please, please," he begs.

"The place was kind of creepy. One man screamed, 'Run!' over and over and over. It freaked me out," I tell him. I'm not ready to talk about the fact that my mother had a meltdown and had to be sedated right in front of my eyes.

"I don't care," Johnny insists. "I want to see it. It sounds cool."

"It is definitely not cool," I say.

"Okay, then—it sounds interesting," Johnny says. "I know your Mom would love me."

I sort of feel that she would, also. "When I decide to bring friends, you will be one of the first," I tell him.

My God! I have seen my mom *one time*, and suddenly everyone wants to go with me, and I don't know if I'm even so eager to go again. How did my friends find out so quickly? I didn't tell anyone. All I did was post a selfie on Snapchat. The photo was of me on the elevated subway that I took home from Coney Island. I thought it was kind of an interesting view. Me, against the window, with the buildings and sky behind me. I guess they figured it out. Maybe the look on my face said it all.

CHAPTER THIRTY-ONE

"What are you doing for Passover?" Zeina asks me the next day.

We are sitting in my bedroom after school. Zeina is unwrapping her hijab, which she only wears at home these days.

"Passover? Why do you care about Passover?"

"Because I am going out with Sam Bernstein."

"Really?"

Now that *is* "crazy" (24). Sam is sort of Orthodox. His parents are modern Orthodox, I know, since Zayde wanted Dad to join Sam's parent's temple, and Dad had said, "No way!"

"I can't believe the two of you are going out. Did your parents go 'crazy' (25) yet?"

"They don't know. Actually, neither does he!"

"What? How are you going out with him if he doesn't know you're going out with him?"

"Prom. I want him to take me to the eighth-grade prom. He's so cute. He's so smart. I am trying to work at this, but I don't know what to do. I figured you would know, since you're a writer, even though you're not writing now. What

(24) Crazy: Not thinking clearly
(25) Crazy: Bonkers

do you think? Should I try to get him to invite me to his Passover dinner?"

"Seder. It's called the Seder, not a Passover dinner. Anyway, what does being a writer have anything to do with anything? And oh, my God, I totally forgot about prom."

"Did you forget about graduation, too?"

"Sort of."

Fortunately, I applied to high schools before I lost my speech, but now I have to think about graduation, the prom, my mother.

"You have to help me to get Sam Bernstein to notice me," Zeina persists.

I make a face. "I don't even have a boyfriend! Why ask me?"

Zeina sighs. "Okay, I guess you are not going to be helpful on this one. Maybe we should ask Ava. I bet she knows how to get a guy to ask her to prom."

"I wouldn't be surprised. You know, it's not a bad idea. You want me to text her?"

"Yeah, ask her if she can meet us at Pino's!"

"I'm sure it's not as hard as you're making it out to be–getting Sam to ask you. Just be yourself."

My phone pings. "Ava says Pino's in fifteen."

"Well, it's a good thing Ava's on the job, because 'Just be yourself' is not helpful, Pilar. I *am* being myself, all day long, and he doesn't know I'm alive."

"Well, fine, we'll figure out a way for you to be yourself, only on steroids. Metaphorically, that is."

"See? That's why I asked the writer! Metaphorical steroids–I love it!"

"And you have to come with me to see my mother."

"Really. You trust me like that?"

"Are you kidding? I trust you more than anyone in the world!"

But is that true? It feels true—even though I never fully realized it until now. So many new things to feel and truths to realize! It's all coming at me very fast.

I look at Zeina and realize that she must be eating again. She's not all skin and bones like she was before. Does that mean that Ramadan is over? Or is it more than that? Is she getting her head together about whatever was bothering her? Is her father feeling better?

Does the fact that I notice mean that I, also, am getting better? I have been so wrapped up in my own trauma that I didn't even notice her gradually putting weight back on until now. Have I been that wrapped up in myself? It seems so.

"You look good," I say, "not so skinny."

Zeina nods and smiles softly. "I'm feeling less nervous," she says. "My appetite returned."

"I'm glad," I say. I hope she will tell me more when she is ready.

"When should we go to see your mother?" Zeina asks.

I'm not sure why I'm going back to see Star—I've decided to call her that instead of Mom; it puts some distance between us, and I need distance. Going back is just something I have to do. I hope having Zeina with me will make it less terrifying if she goes "crazy" (26) again.

"Let me think about it," I say.

(26) Crazy: A wild outburst of deranged thinking

CHAPTER THIRTY-TWO

"Metaphorical steroids? You guys are too much."

Ava shakes out her curls. I'm a little annoyed she is making fun of my metaphorical steroids. I don't see why that wouldn't work.

I slurp my Coke. "Well, you're the expert. Tell us what to do, then, since you know so much."

"Why don't you just ask Sam to go to the prom with you?"

Zeina and I stare at Ava, who is calmly picking the eggplant off her Sicilian slice and popping it in her mouth. We are stunned. This has literally never occurred to us.

"I mean...I guess I could ask him," Zeina stammers. "But what if he says no? Then I'll feel bad!"

"You expect the guy to ask you, but you might say no, right? Aren't you willing to take the same risks as a guy?"

I think about this. I am a feminist—always have been, always will be. I definitely believe there is nothing a man can do that a woman can't do, too. A lot of times, the woman might even do it better. So of course, I know Ava's right—in theory.

I glance at Zeina, who looks panic-stricken. "I wouldn't know what to say," she mumbles.

"Look." Ava puts down her slice. "It's easy. Just practice on me. We'll do it first, so you can get the idea.

Penny–you pretend I'm Sam, and you are asking me to the prom. What would you say?"

I bat my eyes and put on a gooey smile.

"Gee, Sam! You are so much prettier than I've ever seen you before! Did you get hair extensions?"

Zeina dissolves into giggles, but Ava gives me a withering look.

"Very funny. If you don't want to help, why are you here?"

"Okay, okay, I'm sorry! I'll be serious," I say hastily.

"Try again." Ava is not letting me off the hook.

I take a deep breath, trying to photoshop Sam's face over Ava's features. To my surprise, it's easier than I thought. Ava is helping me out by putting on a friendly, attentive expression.

"Hey, Sam," I begin. "I was wondering–do you want to go to the prom?"

"So, that's a good start," Ava says. "But I'd change up the wording a little. You don't want to set yourself up for some version of 'Yes, I do, but not with you,' because then you leave him no choice but to hurt your feelings. Do you see what I mean?"

Now that she puts it that way, I do. It is galling that Ava is telling me, the writer, how to phrase things, but I have to admit it–she's right. I think for a moment, rearranging sentences in my head.

"Hey, Sam. I'm getting a late start on the prom thing–you know, I applied to, like, five-hundred high schools–and I was thinking...if you don't already have other plans, would you like to go with me?"

"Perfect!" Ava approves. "The 'if you don't have other plans' part leaves him an out without him having to be rude about it."

"But I don't want to give him an out. I want him to go to the prom with me!" Zeina protests.

Ava looks severe. "Do YOU want to go out with some dude who doesn't leave you any choice? Some guy who manipulates you into saying yes, when you really wanted to say no?"

Zeina looks like she's about to pop off with, "Yeah, as long as that guy is Sam." Ave gives her a do-not-even-go-there glare. Reluctantly, she mutters, "I guess not."

"Well, neither do they. Fair is fair." Ava turns to Zeina. "Okay, it's your turn."

Zeina twiddles the ends of her hair. "You know what? I don't think this is a good idea. Forget I asked."

"Oh no you don't! Come on–you're up!"

"Fine! Sam, will you go to prom with me, even though you're Jewish and I'm Muslim, which makes us cultural enemies, and this can only end in one way–the tomb scene from *Romeo and Juliet*?"

Ava says, "That was terrible. I can't believe you just asked Sam Bernstein if he'd like to commit suicide in an Italian mausoleum with you."

"Well, it's true! I can't believe a Jewish boy will even consider going out with me!"

Ava sighs. "Listen. Penny is Jewish, and the two of you are BFFs. So knock it off. You are talking about *one night* at the *prom*. A *date*–not a double suicide! And FYI, the prom theme this year is *Over the Rainbow*, not *Carrie*!"

"I'm sorry! I just don't know what to say!"

"Just say the same thing I said," I suggest. I feel bad for Zeina. Ava should know how hard this is.

Zeina composes herself and tries again. "Um. Hi, Sam.

I am thinking of, um, going to the prom, and I thought it might be nice to go with–uh–you. If you're free. Heh."

"Better," Ava approves. "Now, go home and practice that until you leave out all the 'ums' and you don't end on that dopey little giggle. Then park your tray next to him at lunch, or catch him in the hallway and ask!"

Zeina glances at me. "Hallway, I think. If I put my tray down next to him at lunch, then I have to keep talking to him, and that would be really awkward if it turns out he doesn't want to go with me."

I nod emphatically. The hallway seems like a much better bet to me, too.

"Good thinking." Ava is done. She picks up her pizza. Problem solved.

"So, Ava," I say. "You *are* going to go with Calvin, right?"

To my surprise, Ava starts to blush. "I–well, I'm not really sure who I'm going with yet. Me and Calvin–we're kind of taking a break."

"Well, who are you thinking of? Is there anybody else special you like?" Zeina chimes in.

"Um...kind of. I–I'm just not sure yet."

"Well, did you *ask* this guy if *he* wants to go with you?"

"I'm thinking about it."

"So *he* hasn't asked *you*?" I can't believe it.

"He sort of has, and he sort of hasn't."

"Do you want to practice what to say on us?"

Zeina is dying to be helpful. And also dying to know who it is who could get the unflappable Ava this flustered. He must be the hottest guy in the school. Who could it be? Wait–maybe he's not even *IN* our school! Maybe he's a high school student!

"No!" Ava glances at her phone. "Hey, I'm sorry, I have to get going. My-um-my mom wants me to help out with..."

Her voice trails off. She grabs her backpack and heads for the door, calling, "Let me know how it went after you've ask him, huh?" over her shoulder.

I look at Zeina, and see my own skepticism mirrored on her face. "Do you think that text was from her mom?"

Zeina shakes her head. "Nope."

"Me neither."

CHAPTER THIRTY-THREE

I decide that I'm not yet ready to bring a friend to see Star. Now, though, I wish I wasn't alone as I walk down the long hall to my mother's room. Her door is half open and I peer in. She's in a chair looking out the window. I step inside.

"Hi Mom...Star."

Slowly she turns toward me. Wild gray hair haloes her lined face beneath a man's fedora hat. She wears red lipstick and a man's suit jacket that flaps baggily on her thin frame. The "crazy" (27) blankness slides from her eyes as they widen in amazement and she stands.

"Do I know you?" she asks.

"Yes, Star. It's me, Penny."

"My Penny. My beautiful little girl." She reaches for me and slobbers kisses on my face. After she kisses me, she turns back to the window and returns to staring. "What is it like outside?" she asks.

"You never go outside?"

"There is no one to take me."

"Why can't you go yourself?"

She looks at me with those huge green eyes shadowed by the fedora. Dad told me she was fat, but all of that is

(27) Crazy: Empty

done. When I gaze at her I see a person so small, so diminished, and so sad. Just yesterday Dad told me that in therapy he finally shared the story of how the police called him at work to tell him Star was at a Macy's department store, taking off her clothes and screaming, "God is dead! God is dead!" just like she did when I was there. Thankfully, when I visited, she kept her clothes on, though maybe that would have happened next if the nurses hadn't stopped her. So "crazy" (28).

"I'll go outside with you for a walk next time I come. And maybe I'll bring a friend."

But then, right away, I think, *No I won't*, and I feel like a terrible person for having lied to my mom. My poor, sad, mixed-up mom, locked away forever in her small little world.

"Oh, I would love that!" Her face lights up. "Let's go right now!" she says, bouncing out of her chair.

"Oh. Well, I'd love to," I stammer, "but the thing is, I actually have a ton of homework, so this was going to be kind of a short visit. I don't think we probably have enough time today. Besides, don't you have to get permission or anything?"

Her face darkens. "I don't have to get permission for anything! I am the king! I do as I please! And I want to go outside. You promised!"

Oh, my God. What have I started? All I did was ask did she ever go outside, instead of looking out the window all the time.

My mother roots around in her closet. "Where are my clothes? Who took my clothes?" she shouts. "My fur coat–

(28) Crazy: Insane

where is my fur coat?"

She whirls around on me. "You stole it!" she accuses.

"No, I didn't! Ew! I would never take anybody's fur coat. First of all, I'm not a thief. And second of all, I don't believe in murdering animals to turn them into fur coats."

This was the wrong thing to say, I realize when my mother's face turns purple with rage.

"Murderer! Murderer! YOU'RE the murderer! You stole my coat, and you stole my Penny! My baby girl, where is she? You are not my Penny–you are a fake and a thief. You are only pretending to be my Penny so you can come in here and steal from me! What have you done with my daughter? Did you kill her? Is my Penny dead?"

She glares at me with a menacing look on her face. Her screams are so loud that they are drowning out the usual "God is dead" noises in the hallway. I am scared half to death. What if my mother attacks me?

An attendant pokes her head in the door. "What's going on in here? Star, do you need to go to the quiet room?"

"No! I don't want the quiet room! And I am not Star! I am Stavan! King Stavan! This girl, this–imposter–she tried to get me to go outside with her. She's trying to kidnap me, probably wants to do away with me, like she did my Penny! Lock her up! She stole my fur coat; she wants to murder me!"

This is such a total inversion of what really happened that all I can do is stand there gaping at the attendant, who purses her lips and says, "All right, Stavan, I can see you're upset. Now, I'm going to take this young lady away and if you calm down, maybe we won't have to visit the quiet room."

She takes my arm and gently steers me toward the door.

My mother is pacing back and forth, angry and triumphant, muttering, "Lock her away. Lock her away. She's bad, she's bad, have to lock her away. Never let her out. Never let her out."

The attendant waits until we are in the elevator to speak. "I'm sorry you had to see that," she says. "We recently had to change her meds, and sometimes it takes a little while for her to adjust to the new dosage. She should be back to normal by the next time you want to visit. I'm sorry nobody warned you. She's very volatile right now."

Back to normal? My mother will be back to normal? But what does that even mean?

"Thank you," I say. I feel so sad I can hardly stand it. I wonder if I can ever make myself come back.

On the way out, I stop at the nurse's station. A nurse looks up from her work.

"Can I help you?"

I tell her that I'm Star Lasky's daughter and I'd like to know what medication she is currently on. She won't tell me because I'm a minor. She says Dad has to give me a notarized letter before she can give me that info. I confide in her that I just want to know if she'll be calm if I decide to visit. I tell her what happened the last time.

"I'll talk to the doctor and see what I can find out," she says, which isn't exactly helpful, but I thank her anyway.

CHAPTER THIRTY-FOUR

I decide I need reinforcements along next time I go to see my mom. Reinforcements who aren't freaked out by the antics of an unpredictable parent.

"Remember when you promised me you would come with me to see my mom?" I ask Zeina the next day after school.

"Yeah." She is so eager that she is jumping up and down.

"Well, how would you feel about tomorrow after school?"

"Oh, my God, oh, my God, oh, my God!"

Without her hijab, I can really see Zeina's face, and wow! The blue eyes, the black hair. I have been sworn to secrecy that her hijab goes off during the day.

"Look," I say. "Don't get too built up about it. She is kind of... I don't know if she'll be having a good day or not. I'm hoping for the best. Maybe if you're there too, she'll be calmer. And then next week, we can go to Coney Island."

"Coney Island, as in Luna Park, as in rides?"

"Yup."

"My mother would never let me go."

"So don't tell her. I do that sometimes with my dad." What I don't tell her is how wrong it feels.

"It doesn't feel right."

I can tell she is as uncomfortable as I am. Even more. There is so much lying in the world today, that maybe it's *not* the thing to do. It makes the "crazy" (29) world even "crazier" (29).

"Tell your mom, then, and say we're going together. She really trusts me."

That in itself feels "crazy" (30) since I can't even trust myself.

"Are you certain you want to bring a friend?" Dad asks that night at supper. "Sometimes she really goes 'crazy' (31). The medications don't always work."

"What medication?"

"Haldol."

"How do you know that?"

"I called the hospital and spoke to the doctor. He said that her behavior can depend on how long ago she took the medicine. You might get there as it's wearing off. That's probably what happened the last time you went to see her."

"Can he predict when it's safe to go see her?"

"I'm afraid he can't. You just have to take your chances."

The next day, after school, I take Zeina to Mom's, thinking about Dad's warning. I have explained to Zeina what happened during my last visit, and she says she is willing to go anyway. When we arrive, Mom is in her same old spot.

(29) Crazy: deceitful, out of control
(30) Crazy: Insane
(31) Crazy: Bonkers

"Star, it's me—Penny."

She turns around. "You are so beautiful."

"This is Zeina, my friend."

"Hi, Mrs. Lasky."

"Mr. Lasky," Mom corrects her.

"Hi, Mr. Lasky."

Zeina is wearing her hijab today. Is this because she's so far out of her normal territory that she's nervous? Is meeting Mom making her nervous? Probably some of both. Just the same, she moves right into Zeina-saves-the-day mode.

"I love your hat." She points to mom's fedora.

"And I love yours. I am so glad that Penny brought a friend."

"I'm happy to be here."

Zeina, plagued with her own demons, and here she is being so nice to Mom. Nicer than I am. I don't always feel lucky, but with friends I am very lucky.

"What do you like to do, Mr. Lasky?"

"I used to like to fix appliances when I was young. I also like to write."

She gets up, walks over to her mattress and there, under the bed, are hundreds of napkins with scribbles all over them. "The staff allows me to keep these."

Curiosity overcomes my lingering fear that I'll say the wrong thing and set her off again. "Can I take them home?" I ask her.

"Why?"

"I'm a writer, too. Maybe I can combine our stories."

"That would be terrific."

My mom gets very excited and starts piling all the napkins together, higgledy-piggledy. I realize there is no such thing as making sense of what order they are in. Why did I say that thing about writing our stories? To do that, I would have to want to write again, the last thing in the world I want to do now. Still, it might make for a really interesting book, and I start feeling that little prickle of excitement I get when I have a good idea for a story. Besides–I want to read those napkins.

Zeina and I leave, Mom hugging Zeina extra hard. As we walk to the bus, Zeina tells me, "I really like your mom."

"She doesn't make you uncomfortable?"

"I'm used to 'crazy' (32) people."

"Maybe they're not 'crazy' (33) after all. Could it be that their brains are just wired differently?"

"Could be. Who knows?" says Zeina.

We reach the bus stop across from the beach. I check the schedule. Twenty minutes till the next bus. I guess not a lot of people want to come out here. It's twilight; suddenly, I am chilly without the sun. We cross the street and sit quietly on the bench, each of us thinking our thoughts. I finger the napkins in my pocket. Will they explain anything about my mother to me?

"Zeina," I say. "Can I tell you something?"

"Sure." My friend. My *best* friend. I know I can talk to her. Why am I scared to say this? Spit it out, Pilar.

"Sometimes I'm scared I'm going to turn out to be–you know–sick, the way my mother is sick. Do you think that could happen?"

I wait for Zeina's verdict like she has the power to

(32) Crazy: People with mental illness
(33) Crazy: Mentally unstable

change my future.

Zeina sighs. "I don't know. I guess anything *could* happen. To any of us, I mean. I look at my dad, and I worry sometimes that one day I'm going to wake up middle-aged, sitting on a worn-out sofa with tufts coming out of the armrests, staring at nothing on an old television set. If I have enough disappointments in my life–enough setbacks–could that ever be me? I don't know. I *feel* pretty strong. Like, mind over matter, right? I *feel* like I'll always tough out anything bad that happens to me. But maybe my Dad thought that, too." She falls silent. After a minute she adds, "I get the sense you're pretty strong, too. So–no. I don't see you becoming like your Mom."

"But then why did I stop talking? Why am I still seeing a shrink? Zeina, I wound up in the *hospital* because I had a psychotic break!" I'm glad she is reassuring me, but I don't want to let myself off the hook too easily. This is too important.

"Yeah, but now you're talking again. And you are out of the hospital, and back in school. Back to normal. Your Mom–she can't do that. And the reason you're seeing a therapist is you've had a lot to deal with this year. Trust me–if we had good insurance, I'd be seeing one myself. Assuming my nutty dad would let me. He doesn't believe in psychiatry. Figures, right? And guess what. I wasn't eating, right? I know you knew that, but now I am. I figured out starving myself wasn't helping anyone."

"That's awful," I say, and I mean it. For the first time, I am grateful to have my own dad, with his 'there's a specialist for everything that can possibly go wrong with you' approach to life. I wonder if talking to a psychiatrist might help Mr. Mohammed. It has helped me, I have to admit. Hasn't helped my mom, though. It's all so confusing. But maybe the fact that talking to Joaney Shoaney, Queen of Psychobaloney, has actually helped me means I'm really *not* going to be like my mom, after all. I can hope, right? And Zeina knew she's had "food" issues all along.

"You know you can always talk to me, though, right?" I say. "I've had so much therapy at this point that I can probably hang out a shingle and set up my own office."

Zeina giggles. "Help me, Dr. Lasky," she says. "I am obsessed with going to Luna Park and riding a roller coaster. Tell me, what can it mean?"

"It means the bus is here, and it also means that next week we will rid you of your obsession by going to Coney Island and riding the Thunderbolt!" I announce. "That will be five hundred dollars, and you can pay me in cotton candy."

Zeina rolls her eyes. "Penny, you are cra— No. No, I take it back. You're really not."

She fist-bumps me and we move toward our seats. The warmest seat is in the back, so that is where we go.

CHAPTER THIRTY-FIVE

The last day of school before spring break, Reise grabs me in the halls. "Are you writing?"

"Not really." Go *away*, Reise.

"I hope you can begin again. Maybe use this spring break as an opportunity to start again, Penny. You are, after all, a writer.

I don't correct her when she calls me Penny. I am starting to feel more like a Penny, less of a Pilar. I think how I would like to write my mother's story, since I told her I would. Reise doesn't ask me about the play, and she is nervous, unsure around me, sort of the way my dad is. I guess they're afraid they might accidentally say something to make me go mute again. Could it happen? I don't know. Maybe she feels guilty that she stole my play and stopped my voice. Well–she should!

Dad and Reise are not the only ones. Passover is coming up, and I've noticed my cousins Deirdre and Robert hardly call me anymore to make plans. When we see each other, they act like they are scared of saying the wrong thing. I can't blame them. Maybe they're scared that I'm "crazy" (34). But it's not the Seder or writing or time binge my Netflix favorites that I look forward to.

(34) Crazy: Unhinged

It's Coney Island with my friends. It's not the Coney Island where there is a psychiatric facility where the bleach smells bombard me and the stinks of urine and vomit make me ready to puke. It's *my* Coney Island—the sea, the rides, my friends. And mostly there's the ocean: vast and rolling, mysterious and endless sea. At the ocean my mind rests in the rumble of the surf. I love it! I love it! I love it.

Before I know it, after two nights of Seders, too much matzah, too many boring services, I am here in Coney Island once more with Zeina, Ava, Johnny, and—Sam Bernstein. Johnny just shows up, completely out of the blue, with Sam. No forewarning, no explanation. Nothing! Does Johnny know how much Zeina likes Sam?! This is too good to be true! Yet here he is!

Sam and Zeina are already looking each other over.

"Sam, I'm not sure you ever met my friend, Zeina Mohammed. Zeina, this is Sam Bernstein," I jump in with the introduction." They exchange shy hellos.

"I know the two of you like art a lot," I add lamely.

Lame or not, it works. "I *do* like art a lot," says Zeina. "I love it!"

"Me too," Sam says.

"Can I get you a cotton candy?" Zeina asks Sam. "Oops, forgot, Passover."

"No worries. I'm not observant, though I like the holidays. Sure."

"Pink, or blue?" says Zeina. "I'm not observant, either," she adds.

"Doesn't matter. They taste the same. But you're not Jewish. So how do you mean, 'not observant'?"

Zeina blushes; her whole face is red.

"I mean, I'm not an observant Muslim."

Zeina looks really attractive without her headscarf and with her flawless skin and thick, full hair. Her tight jeans are not something her parents would be happy about. But it is what is. We aren't always what our parents dream us to be. Briefly, I wonder what fantasy my mom had about me.

All these serious thoughts leave me as we wait in line for the roller coaster at Luna Park. The Thunderbolt with its twists and turns and a 90-degree vertical drop.

"I'm not going." I quickly get out of the line.

"C'mon!" A chorus erupts from my friends.

"I'm afraid of tight spaces and really scared of heights. Give me a break!"

"Me, too," says Zeina, getting out of line.

"Really?" pleads Sam. "I really wanted to go on this ride with you!"

"Please, Zeina, don't do this for me," I whisper in her ear. "I'm doing it for you. Three's a crowd."

I had counted back the seats and realized that I'd be in the car with them. That definitely wasn't part of my plan.

"Oh–okay, Sam. Since you asked so nicely." She gives Sam a sidelong glance out of those blue eyes of hers, and I can tell—he's a goner. When did Zeina learn to flirt?

Sam grabs her hand. Mission accomplished.

"Hey." Johnny is beside me.

"Why aren't you on the ride?" I ask.

"Like you, those things make me sick."

"Actually, I'm really okay with them," I say with a laugh. "Zeina likes Sam, so I want to give them some alone time."

I glance up at the coaster. Ava, looking a little unhappy,

has been squashed into a car with a large man wearing the obligatory tourist camera around his neck. She sees me looking and waves, then goes back to scrunching over as far away from the tourist as she can get.

Johnny laughs. "You sly devil, P! You must be feeling better. That's the P I know."

"Oh, no!" I say. "I'm the *NEW-NORMAL* me. I was a little kooky before, but no more."

The roller coaster heaves into motion, and the shrieks begin.

"Poor Ava," I say. "I know she'd rather be on the ride with one of us than with him."

"I'll make it up to her on the Ferris wheel," Johnny says. "It's not so much heights that bug me–it's those sudden drops. I don't think Ava would enjoy getting my up-chucked hot dog in her lap."

Before I know it, we're talking about everything—Taylor Swift, K-Pop, Reise, medicine, the president. He is so easy to talk to! I've missed Johnny more than I knew. He is so comfortable with all he has been through.

"We should do our tradition," he says.

"Do we have time? I don't want to make Ava feel like we're ditching her. Zeina, I'm not so worried about–I think she'd *like* us to ditch her just now."

Our tradition is that we go on the baby rides like Dumbo the Elephant and the sailboats together. Johnny and I have been coming to Luna Park together since we were too small to go on anything but the baby rides. We did this when he was Jasmine. He is so much happier now. Why didn't I see this, how important it is just to find happiness? For old times' sake, we always go on one or two of those when we're here together.

"I think we can do just one," I say. "Which one do you want?"

"Teacups. Definitely the teacups."

The teacups have me laughing so hard that I am nearly peeing in my pants. The centrifugal force throws me into Johnny, right onto his lap. I struggle playfully to right myself but it's not so easy. Johnny helps, moving me aside. I'm back in my seat for less than a minute when I realize that he hasn't let go of my hand. Johnny is holding my hand!

Does he even realize it? He must know! He's gazing off in another direction, not even looking at me, but his face has turned pink. Squeezing my hand a little tighter, he turns back to me.

"You really are so cute," he says, turning even redder from ear to ear.

What do I say? I have no idea what to reply.

"I'm sorry," he quickly adds. He starts to pull his hand back but I keep hold of it.

"Why?" I ask.

"I didn't mean to say that. I slipped."

"It's okay. I kind of like the slip." No one ever said that to me, unless you count my dad, who says it all the time—too much!

Johnny nods and keeps hold of my hand, relaxing a little. "Listen, I want to tell you that I'm sorry about your mom."

"You know?"

"Yeah."

"Who told you?"

"Zeina. Who else?"

Yes, who else but Zeina, friend, protector and finally—

great gossip, who I hear screaming from up above, on the Ferris wheel. Bestest of friends.

"Thanks, Johnny." I squeeze his hand harder.

"There's something else," he says. "I don't know how to say this, but–about that time I–you know?"

I nod, and I can feel myself turning red, too. Boy, do I know! I'm flustered. Johnny's hand feels so good in mine–warm and steady. But for me it's the warmth and steadiness of friendship, and I know this.

"Johnny, I need to tell you something," I begin.

"Don't bother. I know already. And I'm not mad—really, truly!"

"I think you are the cutest guy, ever, and I love you beyond, beyond, but not the way you want me to."

"I know that. I get it. And I totally understand."

"You do?"

"Yes. And it's all right. I wanted to tell you I'm sorry I almost messed us up by pushing for something you don't feel. And I know now that I was wrong."

We hug the tightest hug, ever.

"Oh, Johnny. You are the best. And you know, you're pretty cute yourself."

His eyes flash mischief. "You're not the only one who thinks so, P."

"Whaaaat? Are you seeing somebody?" I punch his shoulder. "You'd better not be holding out on me!"

"More will be revealed, so stay tuned," he says.

The teacup slows to a stop. Johnny jumps out and takes off running for the Ferris wheel, where Zeina, Sam and Ava stand waiting for us.

CHAPTER THIRTY-SIX

Now it's Johnny's turn to come with me to visit Mom.

"I really want to do this," he assures me. "Me and your mom are tight," he says, demonstrating with his hands. I've told him about her gender mix-up so Johnny thinks he and Mom must be two-of-a-kind.

"Johnny, my mom has no idea about gender—or maybe she does. She may not be like you. She chooses to be opposites—so one day she is a prince and the next day she is a princess, one day Star, the next day Stavan."

"Sounds cool to me."

When we get to my mom's, he immediately starts singing to her, a song from *The King and I*, "Getting to Know You," and mom joins right in, laughing. Actually laughing. Her face is completely different when she laughs. Bright.

"Call me Star."

"I'm Johnny."

They start chatting, and there is no stopping them. All the parents of all my friends love Johnny, since he is so easy to talk to. Mom tells him about her fantasy of building a race car from scratch.

"Me too," says Johnny.

"What-what?" I sputter.

I know this is bullshit, but then he bends over and

whispers in my ear, "It makes her happy."

"What do you like to do, Johnny?" she asks him.

"Acting. Singing. I am going to be in Penny's play when she finishes it."

"You're writing a play, Penny?"

"Sort of." I give Johnny the evil eye.

"Maybe I can help you finish it," Star exclaims.

"Sure, maybe."

Never.

Johnny has brought life to my mom. She is laughing. She takes that stupid black fedora off her head.

"I am so happy you came to visit me, Johnny," she tells him.

"I am so happy I came, Mr. Lasky."

"Star. Call me Star."

*

"You are the best bullshitter," I tell Johnny, who takes my hand, and swings it, humming "Getting to Know You," while we exit the hospital.

"I'm an actor."

"You're a good one!"

"The best!"

His big, brown eyes sparkle. There is nothing phony about him. He is authentically for real.

"You were so great with my mom."

"I like her." He pauses, then adds, "Though I get what you mean. It's not a gender thing at all–it's her. She just seems...not very tethered to reality."

I think it over. That seems like a good way to put it. "Do you think I might ever...?" I falter.

Johnny hoots. "Are you kidding, P? You are the most grounded person I ever met. For *years* I've been trying to get you to visit an alternative universe, and you just aren't having any. Nope–I'm afraid you are doomed to a lifetime of sanity and utterly boring conformity."

I am really happy for the first time in a long time. "You jerk," I say affectionately. "I'm a writer. I spend half my life in alternative universes."

"Yeah," he says, suddenly serious. "But the difference between you and Star is–you can leave them whenever you like."

And for that I have no answer, because Johnny is right.

CHAPTER THIRTY-SEVEN

Spring break comes and goes so quickly, too quickly. Passover ends, and lots of ice cream, pizza and frozen yogurt. Zeina starts seeing Sam and she is so excited she doesn't have the words for it! I visit my mother, not once, not twice, but three times. Twice she had bad episodes. Once she said I was not her daughter but that I was a space alien who had taken Penelope's form just to trick her. Mostly, though, she was pretty good.

With each visit, I got better at predicting when they had just given her the Haldol. Aside from that one time with Johnny, my mother is mostly quiet. Each time a few more words emerge. Each time she is excited to see me, then seems to lose her words and retreats into the shell of her black pants, long white shirt and black fedora hat. Often she calls me Penelope—she's the only one who uses my formal name. I never tell her about "Pilar" but this name means less and less to me. Today when I see her she says, "How are you?"

I answer, "Not fine."

"Why, sweetheart?"

"I hardly know you. I want to get to know you!"

"Did you read my writing?"

"Not yet." I want to read it but something stops me every time I begin. I suppose I'm afraid of what I might discover about my new-found mother.

She gets up and takes out several boxes. "Read what you got from under my mattress. And read what's inside here. You'll find out about me."

This is "crazy" (35). I thought there were so many scraps of paper beneath her bed, but now there are reams of paper—a whole novel.

"Your dad probably told you a little bit, but there's so much more. And if you read my diary, there's a back story."

"I did read it."

"I figured." She doesn't care. Which is weird in itself. I would for sure care if somebody read my diary without asking me!

"I think I know you," she adds.

"Really?"

"Yes. Smart. Curious. A little sad. Confused. Always digging. Looking for answers."

How could she read me so well?

"And you're not 'crazy,'" (36) she says to me. She knows. She knows how scared I am. Some days she's so normal. Why can't she always be like this?

And then, when I get home, it is Dad—always the same with him. He's still nervous around me, walking on eggshells, nervous that he will say the wrong thing and set me off back into a silent world.

"How was your mom?"

"Just great. Why do you always ask me?"

(35) Crazy: Insane
(36) Crazy: mentally unstable

He starts to sing. "I'm just a Dandelion, a fate I don't deserve."

"No, you're my Dad."

I go into my room. He doesn't follow me. I want to read all these scraps of paper. Maybe there's a story here. Or a play.

*

I sit in bed with a sea of Star's papers all around me. I'm crying. Star has become a real person to me, not just a "crazy" (37) person, or a woman. I want to fill a hole in my life. She's Star Lasky. She's someone who has struggled so hard to be a good person, and to be her own person, but who has this awful, confusing mental illness. Wiping my eyes, it comes to me out of the blue. I know why I couldn't finish the play. I couldn't finish my play because it hurt too much.

Star's papers. My mom's papers. They've pushed it all to the front of my brain.

I had no idea that my play is about the day when the people from the medical facility came to take my mother from our apartment. I was there. I saw her struggling and screaming for them to let her go. I was there when they sedated her and I saw her slump into their arms. I thought they had killed her. I believed I'd seen my mother die. And I would not see her for another decade. I would think she was dead.

And I remember something else. I remember the screams. *My* screams, because strangers had come take

(37) Crazy: Mentally ill

my mom away from me. "No, no, no! Mommy! Don't take my mommy! No!" I remember the helplessness of feeling that nobody was listening to me. I remember my Dad, shushing me, telling me be a good girl, calm down, stop screaming. I remember losing all my words in sobs.

I remember it now. That night Dad held me on his lap and we watched *The Wizard of Oz*. He sang "Somewhere Over the Rainbow" to comfort me. I said nothing. There was nothing to say. My mom was gone, and all my words, all my pleading, hadn't stopped it from happening.

Realizing this isn't easy. I cry until ribbons of snot run down my face and my eyes are scorched and red. I soak my pillow. I feel I'll never stop, and I fall asleep lying on top of my mother's papers.

When I awaken, the light outside is still gray. My eyes are sandy and bloated. My nose is raw. Getting out of bed, I lift the shade. The pinks and golds of dawn bounce off the glass of the windows. Above that a long almond-shaped crack of bright blue sky is getting ever wider.

I couldn't write the end of my play because the end didn't exist. Now the end does exist. It's a next act, anyway. I climb back on my bed, pick up my pen and notebook, and I begin to write.

Crazy No More

I am in a fever of writing these days, but I thought I should come up for air just to tell everyone that I'm alive and well. I am writing my true story and I am writing it as honestly as I know how. It's not an easy story to tell. I have to figure out how to use my words again, and how to NOT make my words knives I might stick in the wrong person's heart. I always knew that the play I've written needed a new ending. What I didn't know—had no idea of—is that it also needed a different beginning. I'm going to add a beginning with the new information I now have. Then I'll give the play the ending that was always missing. What happened after that awful night when Dad sang "Over the Rainbow," each of us wishing that we were over the rainbow, anywhere but there in a Brooklyn apartment filled with grief, trauma, and fear.

CHAPTER THIRTY-EIGHT

"Do you realize we're going to different schools in the fall?"

I look at Zeina and the shock of it registers. "Really?"

"Really! I thought you were taking the test for the science high schools, and I figured we'd both get in. I'm going to Bronx Science."

"I know, I totally spaced the test. I had to finish my play."

"Seriously? I mean, you didn't. Finish it, I mean."

"Yeah, and then I got sick. I really couldn't wrap my brain about studying for the test anyway. I ended up applying to a few schools in Brooklyn and that writing school in Manhattan, and fortunately I got into the writing school."

Zeina looks sad. I feel really sad, too.

"Don't forget, I had a nervous breakdown. That's practically a job requirement for writers."

For some reason, this makes me laugh, and Zeina starts laughing, too. We are laughing so hard we are practically peeing in our pants.

"Yeah? And what's the job requirement for us science geeks?"

"Pointy Vulcan ears!" We are rolling on the floor now. My stomach hurts from laughing.

Zeina sits up, wiping her eyes. "So, the prom."

"Yes, the prom. What about it?"

"Sam asked me."

"Ahhh!" I scream so loud that Zeina has to shush me. "I knew it; I knew it!"

"Problem—Mom does not want me to go to the prom since Dad is in one of his moods again. He went on another interview and didn't get the job, so we are all walking on eggshells. I have explained repeatedly that going to prom together does not necessarily imply 'married with children together' but it's like talking to a wall. My mom just keeps saying over and over that we can't afford to get my Dad any more upset than he already is."

I mull it over. "I have an idea."

"What? I know you are always good at ideas. Tell me, Pilar."

"You can call me Penny again."

"Wow, Penny. I like calling you by your real name. It's been so long."

"I think I like being called by my real name, though I'm not sure."

"What do you mean?"

"I'm not sure."

"Well, if you're not sure, I am surely not sure."

Again, the laughter. Hysterical laughter.

"So, what's your idea?"

"Well, I want to go, but I don't want to try and scrounge up a date. How about if I come along with you and Sam? Don't worry-I'll know when to make myself scarce. Your Mom might go for that."

Zeina thinks it over. "Well, I'd have to ask Sam if he's cool with it. But I think you're right—if we go as a group, maybe my Mom will be okay with it. It's a plan!" She hugs me ecstatically.

But still, I am so sad, thinking about me and Zeina going to different schools. I can't imagine not seeing her every day. The therapist I sometimes see—yes, I agreed with Dad, periodically, to go to her office—says it's good to open my horizons; I have been with mostly the same group of kids for eight years. I like them. I love them. And meeting my mom has opened my horizon way larger than anyone can imagine. I could just about fall off the horizon.

I hug Zeina back, really tight, like I will never let her go.

"Surprise." That Monday, Johnny sneaks up on me in the cafeteria. "I have a surprise," Johnny says, pulling the chair beside me. That's Johnny! So dramatic.

"I have a surprise, too. I'm going to the prom with Zeina and Sam." Johnny shouldn't think all the good stuff only happens to him.

"Awesome! You figure out yet what you're wearing?"

"My Wonder Woman outfit." I stick out my tongue.

"Fine, be that way. Well, my surprise is bigger."

Always bigger. Always better. So dramatic. And I know there are still problems at home. His Dad is sometimes out of the picture because it is not so easy for him to have his Jasmine be a Johnny now. He still gets me annoyed sometimes. If I didn't love him so much, I wouldn't love him. But—I do.

"What's your news?" I say.

"I'm going to prom, too."

"Yeah?" So? Of course Johnny's going to prom. How could he not?

"You haven't asked me who I'm going with."

I heave a sigh. Johnny loves to drag it out.

"Pardon my unforgivable lapse. WITH WHOM are you going to the prom, Johnny?" I only turn into a grammar nerd when I truly want to get on his nerves.

"I asked Ava." Having delivered his bombshell, Johnny leans back on his chair and gives me his cockiest grin.

"Wow!"

I am not just surprised; I am shocked. Ava is as girly-girl as they come. And Johnny is Johnny. I start to think about stereotypes. What do I know about anyone, anything. People think of me as a writer, and the only thing I've written in the past few months is my blog—if that counts for anything.

"And?" I prompt.

"And she's coming—as my date!"

"That is great, Johnny."

"And something else." He looks even cockier, if such a thing is possible.

"What?"

"She kissed me."

"No!"

"Yeah!" He breaks into an uncontrollable smile—a real one this time.

"That is great, Johnny. I am so happy for you."

"Thanks!"

There is a pause. I can't think of what to say. Johnny fills it in. "I'm happy you're happy for me."

"I am. Happy for you. It's great, Johnny."

I feel like an idiot. Surely there is another sentence in the English language? Right now, I can't think of one.

I am glad Johnny doesn't have X-ray vision into my brain, since I'm not really that happy at all. I've never been kissed. Not really. Not unless I'm counting the one Johnny planted on me that time, which, honestly, I don't count at all. That one was a mistake–a mistake between friends. I have decided I am not going to go through the rest of my life thinking of my first kiss as a "mistake." I'm talking about a real kiss, a kiss from somebody I've been dreaming about kissing back.

Maybe a little of what I am feeling shows on my face, though. Because Johnny takes my hand, suddenly very serious, and says, "I just have to tell you–I really owe you one."

"Oh?" I can't imagine what he's talking about.

"Yeah." He tips his chair back down and plants his feet on the floor. "See, I've been thinking a lot about what you said. That time when–you know. When I kissed you, and you got so mad at me?"

I am embarrassed. "Oh, forget about it. Ancient history,"

"See, but that's the thing. I don't WANT to forget about it. Because what you said about how I should have asked you first–that stuck with me. It made me mad, at first, but I kept thinking about it. How upset you were, and how I almost wrecked things between us because I took it for granted that you wouldn't mind, so I just went ahead and did it. And I realized I was wrong. So then—"

"Yeah?"

"When I asked Ava to go to the prom with me and she said she would, I was so happy, I wanted to kiss her right then and there. But then I thought about the look on your face that day, and how awful I felt, and how I'd never meant to hurt you or make you cry. So instead, I asked Ava, 'Okay if I kiss you?'"

I stare at this amazingly changed Johnny. "Go on. THEN what happened?"

Johnny blushes. "So then Ava said, 'How about if I kiss you?'"

I am in shock. I am in envious awe of Ava, the girl who will ask the guy for what she wants and not feel like she can't do that. I am incredibly happy for Johnny, who is beaming at me like he just won the lottery.

I am thinking that when I'm finally ready and the right guy comes along, maybe this kissing business will not be as hard to arrange as I think.

*

Here's the big news. The school has scheduled another Awards Ceremony since the other one was so unexpectedly cut short by me.

"Randi would like to come to the Awards Ceremony," Dad tells me.

I know they've been dating though we really haven't talked about it. When I give him no response, he clears his throat.

"I like her," he says.

"I like her, too." At least, I used to. But I'm not interested in a stepmother. No way!

"And she likes you. She wants to be there for you."

I look into Dad's pained eyes and relent. "Sure, why not?" I can think of a lot of reasons why not. But I keep them to myself.

Why can't my mom come? Maybe I'd be embarrassed. Maybe I *am* embarrassed—that my Dad is coming with a date.

*

The night of the awards when we get to the school and I see Randi in front, I shiver, but then end up giving her a big kiss. I have to admit, it's convenient she saved us good seats.

"Glad to see you," I tell her.

I realize I have bigger things to worry about: the prom, graduation, the summer job as a camp counselor that I've applied for, finishing my play, my mother.

Zeina arrives, arm-in-arm with her parents. Her dad is smiling. She is wearing her hijab and she looks beautiful. "Hello, Penny," Mrs. Mohammed says.

"Penny, I remember you!" Mr. Mohammed puts his large hand in mine, shaking it generously. He has the same big, beautiful eyes as his daughter, only I never noticed this before.

Johnny's parents, Mr. and Mrs. Levin, are walking in together—for now—but I know they have been separated. They are both pretty conservative, but Johnny's mom is not about to lose her son. They love Johnny and really— what else matters?

"Did you notice Zeina's hijab?" Mrs. Mohammed asks me. I turn around—Zeina is wearing a rainbow scarf for a hijab. Colors of pride. She did this for Johnny. She did this for other friends of ours.

"I know what it means," Mrs. Mohammed adds when I look at her nervously.

"Does your dad know?" I whisper in Zeina's ear.

"He does." Zeina has a look on her face I have never seen there before, and I realize that she is proud–proud of her dad.

"Do you like my headscarf?" I ask her. I have Grandma's purple scarf tied around my head, Rhoda Morgenstern style. What do I care if it's quirky and no longer worn? It looks good on me. I might even start a trend. I'm happy I don't feel the need to be Miss Super-Normal anymore. What a bore that would be!

Zayde and Grandma are with Dad and Randi across the lobby. We'll go out with them later for supper at Chili's. Zayde waves to me. Grandma smiles when she notices my scarf and sends a thumbs-up. I run to hug them.

And with that we are whisked into the auditorium. Ms. Reise's on stage, looking all proud and everything. After a short speech, she begins.

"Best performer—Johnny Levin."

Cheers from the audience. Mrs. Levin is wiping away tears.

"Our math and science award winner—Zeina Mohammed."

"Yes. Yes. Yes."

Confetti is thrown in the air. That has to be Johnny. Mr. Mohammed is stamping his feet. Mrs. Mohammed looks happier than I ever dreamed she could.

"And for our Writer-in-Residence, the girl who will one day have her plays performed everywhere—Penelope Lasky."

As I go to the podium, I know I am supposed to make a speech, yet all I can come out with is a meek "Thank you!" I smile, since that is what I am supposed to do. And I know that things are changing for the better.

MY PLAY

Here is the end of my play that you've been waiting for: I added to the beginning. I showed a family struggling with the mental illness of the mother. I added a scene where the mother is taken away to the psychiatric facility. After the "Over the Rainbow" scene, I added this:

****

THE BIRTH OF A STORY

Background: Piper, the main character is now thirteen. She has stopped talking. For three months she doesn't talk, rarely writes, and mostly stays in her own little cocoon.
Dad: And I guess there's no denyin'; I'm just a dandelion, a fate I don't deserve.

(Piper, after months of silence, starts laughing.)

Dad: She's alive!

Piper: I am.

Dad: What happened to your voice for the last three months? I've been so worried.

Piper: It disappeared.

Dad: How did you get it back?

Piper: It happened like magic. Do you believe in magic, Dad?

Dad: Not sure.

Piper: I know, you're a scientist.

Dad: I like to think there is a logic behind why things happen a certain way.

(Piper starts crying. Dad reaches over to touch her. She balks at his touch!)

Dad: What's wrong?

Piper: You have no idea, do you?

Dad: Yes, I do. I am so sorry I allowed them to use your play. I was so wrong. I just wanted what was best for you.

Piper: I think I am the only one to know what's best for me.

Dad: Not always.

Piper: There is something else!

Dad (Look of panic across his face): What?

Piper: The diary.

Dad (guiltily): What diary?

Piper: Really, dad, c'mon.

Dad: I have no idea what you're talking about.

Piper: Mom's diary. Mom is alive.

Dad (Looking terrified): How did you know?

Piper: In the drawer, Dad. I was looking for money. For food. You didn't leave me any food money.

(Silence. Silence. Silence)

Piper: Talk, Dad. Do you have Selective Mutism, too?

(Uncomfortable laughter)

Dad: You weren't meant to see it.

Piper: But I did.

Dad: Why did you go through my drawcr?

Piper: Why did you tell me my mother had died?

Dad: I wanted to protect you.

(Silence. More silence.)

Piper: Even if I knew my mother was schizophrenic, at least I would know I had a mother.

Dad: But she was dangerous to you when you were little.

Piper: How?

Dad: Don't make me do this, Piper?

Piper: Well, now I know about her.

Dad: What can I do to make this up to you?

Piper: Where is she now? Her name is Stavan.

Dad: Her name is Star, but she calls herself Stavan. It's a Hindu name, a boy's name. It means "worship."

Piper: Hindu? But we are Jewish. And—does she want to be a man?

Dad: Sometimes. That's why she calls herself Stavan. But she also wants to be a king, a princess, a plumber.

Piper: I don't understand.

Dad: She's schizophrenic. Her disease speaks for her. She is filled with conflicts. And she hears voices.

Piper: I am so mad at you for lying to me.

Dad (Looking down on the ground): I understand.

Piper: Look in my eyes, Dad. That is what Joan, the therapist, always said to me.

Dad (looking in Piper's eyes) How can I make it up to you?

Piper: Where is my mother?

Dad: In a home for psychiatric patients.

Piper: Where?

Dad: In Coney Island.

Piper: I want to visit her.

Dad: Okay, I will go with you.

Piper: No, I will go alone.

Dad: I don't know.

Piper: Now you have to listen to me. I will go alone. You can drop me off.

Dad (Looking sad): Okay.

Act IV

Dad: Are you sure you're okay?

Piper: As okay as I will ever be.

Dad: Call me if you need anything.

(Piper walks into the facility. There is a look of fear on her face. Smells bombard her immediately. And the sounds are haunting. People are screaming. Piper goes up to front desk, the nurse's station. It is locked and guarded.)

Piper: I am looking for Star Lasky.

Nurse: You mean Stavan.

Piper: Yes, I know her other name.

Nurse: And who are you?

Piper: Her daughter.

Nurse (puzzled look on her face): Can I see your identification? (Piper takes out her school ID with a picture on it.) Nurse fills out a slip of paper, goes to the gate, and opens it up. Piper slowly walks down the hall, feeling frightened. Is it the people here, some of whom look overly-medicated, a little scary? Or is it her mother?

When Piper walks into the room, she gazes a small, frail woman sitting by the window. She recalls how her father had said the woman was much heavier. She is wearing a man's fedora and does not move, even though the girl's footsteps are heavy, purposefully.

Piper: Hi.

Star/Stavan (turns around to gaze head-on into the girl's face): Hi.

Piper: It's me, Mom

Star/Stavan (Look of shock on her face): I did have a daughter. She is over thirteen years old. But that was a long time ago.

Piper: It's me, Mom. Piper. I am thirteen.

Star/Stavan (face registers shock, then joy): Is this my beautiful, Piper? My baby girl?

Piper: Not a baby anymore, but it is me, Mom.

Star/Stavan: Let me hug and kiss you. (Tears roll down her eyes.)

(Piper allows herself to be smothered in her mother's embrace)

Star/Stavan: Wait! This is all too much for me! I don't feel well. I hear the voices in my head.

Piper: It's all right, Mom. I'll call the nurses for your medicine. You will be better soon.

Mom: Piper, my darling, my sweetheart. I have been waiting for you my whole life—well, your whole life. Thirteen years. I knew you would come. It is time to tell the world my story!

Piper: I'll tell it for you, Mom. I'm a writer and I want to write the truth because when the truth is told, everyone has a voice.

Crazy For You

No more searching for the meaning of "crazy" (38). I have an idea. This is the last crazy—I think! You will soon see why.

So this is a new blog to mark a new school and new life. I want all my followers—old and new—to know this is NOT a happily ever after story, since I'm not one for sickly sweet sap. All of us have many sides. And the world? So many sides I can't begin to count them.

Today may be a good day, but tomorrow may not.

If this sounds "crazy" (38) to you, you probably shouldn't think about being a writer. Hey, let's face it: words are vast and wild. And the stories that use them are, too. Lately I've started writing poetry again. Here's one that comes from my heart:

What if

The girl in you wakes up a boy
The next day,
   The boy decides to discard his Adidas
   For hot pink Mary-Janes,
   Your mother
   Morphs into your father,
   And your father
   Dreams his way out of this drama,

Do you dismiss?
These "crazy" (38) confusing ways

Or do you stretch out of the box
That was broken anyway
Because the only normal you know
Is you will wake up tomorrow
And the world will always welcome you!

(38) Crazy: Absurd, erratic, preoccupied, impractical, obsessed, silly, annoying, kooky, bizarre, odd, ridiculous, topsy-turvy, passionate, angry, weird, nuts, upside-down, askew, full of cracks, mental, mentally ill, mentally unbalanced, mad, deranged, certifiable, insane, motivated to exasperation, unstable, out of one's mind, maniacal, unexpected, surprising, out-of-control, wild, wild, wild, wild, wild, wild, wild, wild—more every day!

ACKNOWLEDGMENTS

Thanks to all the people who have made this book possible—those who have made my story! It all began with my tribe, Solomon and Mary Laskin, who had four children, all of whom had children. My story also began with the Novick family and my mother, Sylvia Novick, a woman whose mental illness I never understood as a child. What I did recognize in Sylvia, my mother, is she had polar opposites inside her, and that the two sides were at battle—she was a man and a woman, sweet and on fire. I often wondered, not when I was Penny's age, but as I got older, if her schizophrenia was also a result of not being allowed to be herself—or even figure out who that self was. I wish I could have been kinder to her when she was younger, but I am not guilty because I was a kid, and sometimes it is just what kids do.

My mom kept a diary. The story here is just a part of it. Much of this is fiction, though aspects of the characters are not, particularly Penny, who wanted to be a writer and set about trying to discover how to make it happen. Though she (I?) never had Selective Mutism, I had other psychological ways of acting out my anger and confusion. And I always had eclectic friends with their own set of family issues helping me along in this journey.

Thank you to Dana Rae Vessio, who supplied me with all the facts about Selective Mutism. She is in the mental health field, and she was also a student in my graduate Children's Writing class. Dana supplied a multitude of information about this diagnosis, and said she was grateful that a little-known psychological condition was being brought to light. She, too, has a book about mental illness, and I am going to make certain that book has a home down the pike.

Thank you, Karen Clark, a certain fairy godchild, who was able to look at this book with revision in mind, and was able to provide the magic in its revision that I just couldn't. She is a brilliant writer and editor.

Every book has a great editor; I had three. Ira Reiser, my husband, is the best proofreader and an amazing critical reader. Suzanne Weyn, my editor and a friend, approached this book as if it were her own precious baby. Thank you, Suzanne, forever and a day. Thank you, Amanda Reiser, for being tech savvy and helping me with the book in this way. You are a wonderful member of the family.

Thank you to Janet, my Zeina, who is always a part of any chapter. So are all my wonderful friends, who are in this book, and not. And so is my family. One day Ella and Jacob will have their own stories to tell. I am certain that they will be richly complex and also happy!

Thanks to RF CUNY, grant cycle 50, for giving financial support for completion of this book. This book's central focus is about mental illness. It is terrifying to feel you might be "askew" and there is an awful stigma for the child of a mentally ill parent. One of the things I hoped to dispel was the stigma around this illness, by focusing on the many sides in all of us, implying we all have that part of us that lives outside the norm. We all live in the shades of gray, and there are many shades of gray inside all of us. I have learned to accept the two faces that exist in me, and have come to understand mental illness so differently as a result, which is not to say it is not real, and that the reality isn't frightening. Just imagine what it must feel like for the person living with it every day.

Finally, this is a book about being a writer. Everyone has a story that's important, and when you decide to tell it, the world will open its ears wide.

ABOUT ATMOSPHERE PRESS

Atmosphere Press is an independent, full-service publisher for excellent books in all genres and for all audiences. Learn more about what we do at atmospherepress.com.

We encourage you to check out some of Atmosphere's latest releases, which are available at Amazon.com and via order from your local bookstore:

The View From My Window, a novel by Patricia J. Gallegos
Wake Up, a novel by Alejandro Marron
The Dead Life, a novel by Matthew Sprosty
And the Stars Kept Watch, a novel by Peter Friedrichs
Ways and Truths and Lives, a novel by Matt Edwards
The Northern Line, stories by Mike Lee
Madeleine: Last French Casquette Bride in New Orleans, a novel by Wanda Maureen Miller
Ignite, a novel by Marie A. Wishert
Adam's Roads, a novel by Edwin Litts
Heir to the Silver Cross, a novel by Chris Perry
Letters I'll Never Send, a novel by Nicole Zelniker
Somebody's Watching You, a novel by Robin D'Amato
A Gang of Outsiders, a novel by Bobby Williams
The First Great American Novel: Where Parallel Lines Meet (A Story of Non-Sequiturs), by Mathew Serback
No Way Out, a novel by Betty R. Wall
The Saint of Lost Causes, a novel by Carly Schorman

ABOUT THE AUTHOR

Pamela L. Laskin teaches graduate and undergraduate children's writing at City College, where she directs The Poetry Outreach Center. Her book, *Ronit and Jamil,* a Palestinian/Israeli *Romeo and Juliet,* was published in 2017 by Harper Collins, and was on *Entertainment Weekly's* 35 books to have on your radar. *BEA,* a picture book, was a finalist for the Katherine Paterson Prize. She is the winner of Leapfrog's International Fiction Prize for *Why no Goodbye,* published in 2019.

Follow her on Twitter @RonitandJamil, and follow her blog at http://PamelaLaskin.blogspot.com.

www.ingramcontent.com/pod-product-compliance
Lightning Source LLC
Chambersburg PA
CBHW032014050726
47590CB00006B/2166